17

JUNIOR

CLASSICS

Published by
Rupa Publications India Pvt. Ltd 2016
7/16, Ansari Road, Daryaganj
New Delhi 110002

*Sales centres:*
Bengaluru Chennai
Hyderabad Jaipur Kathmandu
Kolkata Mumbai Prayagraj



This is a work of fiction. Names, characters, places and incidents are either the product of the author's imagination or are used fictitiously and any resemblance to any actual person, living or dead, events or locales is entirely coincidental.



P-ISBN: 978-81-291-3951-1
E-ISBN: 978-81-291-4324-2

Third impression 2023

10 9 8 7 6 5 4 3



Printed in India

# Contents

# The Adventure of the Beryl Coronet

Arthur Conan Doyle

'Holmes, look at that madman running down the street,' I said, looking out of the window one morning. The man was in his fifties, tall, very well-dressed and was running through the snow-filled street.

'What do you think is wrong with him?' I asked.

'Is he looking at house numbers?' Sherlock Holmes answered, not even looking up from his newspaper. 'He's coming to see me.'

He was right. Five minutes later, the man was in our room, out of breath but visibly upset. Holmes sat him down and offered him some tea. The man eventually calmed down and told us his story.

'My name is Alexander Holder of the banking firm Holder & Stevenson,' he started. 'Maybe you have heard of me?'

Holmes and I both nodded. Mr Holder was the vice-president of Holder & Stevenson, the second largest bank in London.

But why did he look so worried?

'The circumstances which bring me here would not only disgrace me and the bank, they would also cause a national scandal,' Mr Holder said.

I noticed Holmes leaning forward with interest.

'You are aware that our bank gives out loans, of sometimes very large amounts, against security such as art and jewellery?' Mr Holder asked.

Holmes and I nodded.

Our visitor continued, 'Yesterday, a man—I cannot tell you who it was, but I can tell you that he's very famous—came to see me at the bank. He said he needed a loan of £50,000, and that he preferred to get it from a bank, rather than from friends.

'I asked him how long he needed the money for,' our visitor went on. 'He only needed it for four days, but he wanted it immediately. I said I could give him the money myself, but he insisted on a bank loan and gave me a jewel case as security.

'When I opened the case, I was shocked,' Mr Holder continued. 'It was the Beryl Coronet.'

The crown is a national treasure—thirty-nine enormous beryls covered in solid gold—worth at least twice as much as the mysterious man needed.

'I asked if he was sure he wanted to leave the coronet,' Mr Holder said. He replied that he was, since he would be claiming back it soon. I gave him the money and he left, asking that I not disclose his visit to anyone.

'I decided to take it home with me, rather than leaving it in the bank safe, which could be stolen,' Mr Holder said.

Here, he stopped to tell us about his household. He had four maids whom he trusted completely. Three had been in his employment for many years, while the fourth—a pretty girl named Lucy—had joined just a few months ago.

Mrs Holder had died a long time ago, and so the only other people at the Streatham house were Mr Holder, his son Arthur, and Mary, his niece whom Mr Holder had adopted as a child.

'For a long time, I thought Arthur would follow in my footsteps,' Mr Holder went on, 'but he turned out to be disappointment. When he was young, he became friends with some youngsters with expensive habits. He began gambling and losing heavily and would often beg me to give him an advance on his allowance to give back his debts.

'Arthur often tried to change, but he kept getting pulled back by one of his friends, Sir George Burnwell.

'Arthur was impressed by Sir George,' Mr Holder said. 'He is worldly, a brilliant talker, and very good-looking. It can be hard to resist his appeal. However, I do not trust him, and neither does Mary.'

He then described Mary, calling her his 'right hand' and the 'sunbeam' in his house. According to Mr Holder, Mary had gone against his wishes just once—when she refused to marry Arthur, who was devoted to her.

'Now that you know about my household, Mr Holmes, let me tell you why I am here,' Mr Holder said.

'Last night, during dinner, I told Arthur and Mary about my amazing day,' he said. 'Lucy was just leaving the room at the time. Arthur and Mary wanted to see the crown but I told them I did not want to take it out from my locked drawer in the study.

"I hope the house isn't robbed tonight," Arthur said. "The key of the kitchen storage cupboard fits that lock. I was five years old when I figured that out."

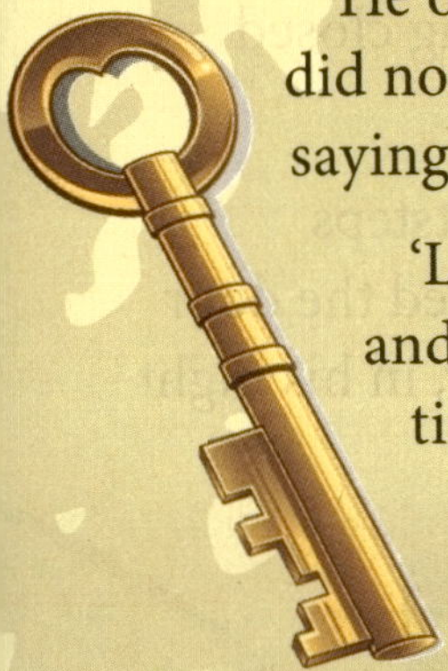

'He often said wild things like that, so I did not pay any attention to what he was saying,' Mr Holder said.

'Later, he followed me into my study and asked me for £200—for the third time this month. When I angrily told him I wouldn't give him another penny, he bowed and went away.

'When he was gone, I checked that the coronet was still in the drawer and re-locked it. Then I started to go around the house to secure the doors and windows. Mary usually does that, but I wanted to be sure,' Mr Holder said.

'As I was coming down the stairs, I saw Mary closing the window and locking it. She looked a little worried.'

"Did you give Lucy permission to go out?" she asked.

'I said no, and she said she had seen Lucy coming in through the back door. She guessed that Lucy had been talking to someone near the gate.'

'I said I would speak to Lucy about it the next morning and went to bed.'

'I did not sleep well since I was worried about the coronet. At about two o'clock in the night, I heard a low sound, like a window being closed gently,' Mr Holder said.

'Suddenly, I heard the sound of footsteps coming from my study. I went in, opened the door and switched on the light to see Arthur, in his night clothes, holding the coronet. It looked like he was using all his strength to bend it.

"Arthur!" I yelled, "You thief!" Mr Holder said.

'When I shouted out, Arthur dropped the coronet, and turned pale. I snatched it and looked at it, and found that one of the gold corners,

with three beryls in it, was missing.

"Villain," I shouted, "You have destroyed it! Where are the jewels which you have stolen?"

"Stolen?" he asked. "Nothing's been stolen. There cannot be any missing."

"There are three missing!" I said. "And you know where they are. Are you a liar as well as a thief? Did I not see you trying to break off another piece?"

'Arthur suddenly became calm. "You have already decided I am guilty. So I will not say another word. I will leave your house in the morning," he said quietly.

'I was half-mad with despair. "You are not going anywhere!" I cried,' Mr Holder said.

'By then, I had woken up the entire household with my shouting. Mary was the first to reach the room. On seeing Arthur and the coronet, Mary fainted in shock. I sent for the police. Arthur stood by sadly.

Arthur asked if I planned to have him arrested. I answered that since the destroyed coronet was national property, it was a public matter and that I would let the law take its own course.'

Holmes had stayed silent all this time. Now he leaned forward and interrupted Mr Holder.

'What did Arthur say to that?' Holmes asked.

'He said he wanted to go out for five minutes. He said it would be helpful to me and to him,' Mr Holder said, 'I shouted, "Why should I let you leave? So that you can hide what you've stolen?" Then I remembered that this could become a national scandal, and begged him to avoid it. All he had to do was tell me where he had hidden the three missing beryls.

"You were caught in the act. Nothing you can say will change anything. However, if you do admit and tell us where you hid the stones, you will be forgiven," I told Arthur. But he just said, "Keep your forgiveness for someone who asks for it," and then he went back to being silent,' Mr Holder said.

'The inspector arrested Arthur and the rest

of us spent the night searching for the gemstones, but did not find them.'

Mr Holder continued, 'This morning, I completed the legalities at the police station and then came here. The police have no idea what to do. I have already offered £1,000 as a reward. You may spend as much as you see fit but I want you to get to the bottom of this. I've lost my honour, my gems and my son, all in one night!'

He sank back into his chair, held his head between his hands and began to rock back and forth, like a tortured child.

Holmes sat silent for a few minutes, with his brows knitted and his eyes closed. Suddenly, he opened his eyes and looked at Mr Holder.

'Do you have many guests?' he asked.

'Just my partner, Mr Stevenson,

and his family. Occasionally, one of Arthur's friends comes over. Sir George Burnwell has been visiting quite often lately. No one else, I think.'

'Do you go out much?' Holmes asked.

'Arthur does. Mary and I are not fond of it, so we stay home.'

'That's unusual in a young girl,' my friend pointed out.

'She's a quiet girl, but she's also not that young. She's twenty-four years old.'

'This business with the coronet … you say it shocked her?' Holmes asked.

'Terrible! It has affected her even more than me,' Mr Holder replied.

'And both of you are convinced that your son is guilty?' Holmes asked.

'I saw him with the coronet in his hands! How can we have any doubts?' Mr Holder.

'That's hardly clear proof. Was the rest of the crown damaged in any way?' Holmes asked.

'Yes, it was twisted,' Mr Holder said.

'Do you not think, then, that your son was trying to fix it?'

'So you think he could be innocent! Thank you! But if he were innocent, why would he not say something?' Mr Holder asked.

'Precisely. If he were guilty, why did he not invent a lie? This case has several interesting points. What did the police think was the noise that you heard?'

'They thought it was probably Arthur closing his bedroom door.'

'As if a man robbing a house would slam a door hard enough to wake people up!' Holmes interrupted. 'And what do they say about the missing gems?'

'They are still going over the house and garden with a fine-tooth comb,' Mr Holder answered.

'My dear sir,' Holmes said, 'do you still not see the confusion of the matter? For instance, if your son took the trouble of going to your study, unlocking the drawer, taking out the coronet, breaking off a part and hiding the gems so cleverly that no one can find them, why would he return to your study where you could find him? Does that make any sense to you?'

'But what else can it be? If he were innocent, why did not explain himself?' Mr Holder asked, bewildered.

'It is up to us to find out,' replied Holmes. 'If you please, let us go to your house and look around.'

'Watson,' he called to me, 'you should come too.'

I didn't argue. I also believed that Mr Holder's son was guilty. However, being familiar with Holmes's skills, I was dying to find out why he thought otherwise.

We took a short train ride, and then an even shorter walk to get to Mr Holder's house. Holmes did not say anything the whole way there, but sat deep in thought. However, Holmes's interest in his case had cheered the banker up greatly.

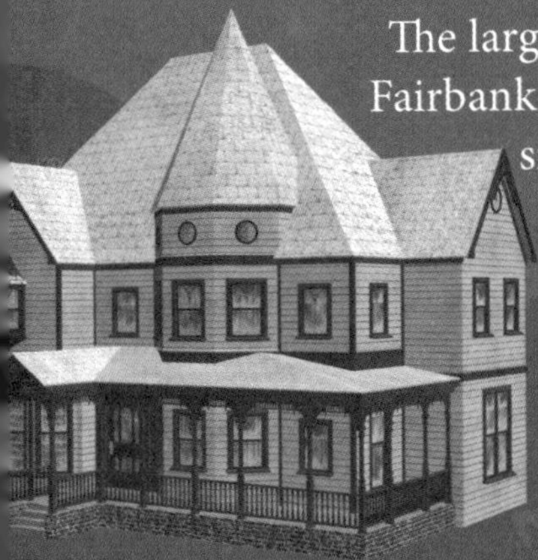

The large house was called Fairbank. A carriage driveway and a snow-clad lawn lay between the road and the iron gates. To its right, a narrow path stretched from the road to the kitchen door. To the left, ran a little-used lane, which led to the stables.

'Is Arthur going to be set free?' Mary asked Mr Holder as we entered.

'No, Mary,' he replied.

'I am sure he's innocent,' Mary said, 'I am sure that you will find him innocent, and then you'll regret having acted so harshly.'

'If he were innocent, why would he not say something?' Mr Holder asked.

'Who knows?' asked Mary. 'Maybe he got angry because you doubted him.'

'How could I not suspect him when I saw him with the coronet?' Arthur's father asked, again.

'Maybe he had just picked it up to look at it?' suggested Mary.

'Whatever the reason, you must believe he is innocent. I cannot bear to think of Arthur in prison!'

'Your affection for Arthur is blinding you to his faults, but I cannot rest till the gems are found. In fact, I've brought a consultant detective to get to the bottom of this,' Mr Holder said.

'This man?' Mary asked, turning to me.

'No, his friend. He wanted to look around by himself. He's in the stable lane right now,' Mr Holder replied.

'What does he hope to find there?' Mary asked, raising her eyebrows as she spotted Holmes enter.

'I hope that you will succeed in proving that Arthur is innocent, sir,' she said.

'Miss Mary Holder, I presume,' Holmes said, adding, 'I hope to prove just that, although I might need a little help from you.'

'I would do anything to help clear up this mess.'

'Did you hear anything last night?'

'I heard my uncle shouting and then came down.'

'You shut the windows and doors. Did you check that they were locked?'

'Yes.'

'Were they all locked this morning?'

'Yes.'

'You said to Mr Holder last night that one of your maids had been out to see her suitor?'

'Yes,' Mary replied. 'She was the girl serving us dinner, so she may have heard uncle tell us about the coronet.'

'I see,' Holmes said. 'You think the girl told her sweetheart about the coronet and that they planned the robbery.'

'Why are you wasting time with unclear theories, when I have already said that I found Arthur holding the coronet?' interrupted Mr Holder impatiently.

'Wait a little, Mr Holder, we'll get back to that shortly,'

said Holmes. 'Now, Miss Holder, you saw the girl return through the kitchen door, I presume?'

'Yes, I had gone to see if the door was locked when I caught her sneaking in. I saw the shadow of a man, as well,' Mary said. 'He is the greengrocer from whom we buy our vegetables.'

'He stood a little away from the door?' Holmes asked.

'Yes, he did.'

'And this man has a wooden leg?'

Mary looked shocked, almost afraid.

'How do you know that?' she asked.

Holmes did not answer her, but instead said he wanted to go upstairs to the study.

'I need to take another look outside,' Holmes said, 'Maybe I should take another look at the ground-floor windows before I go upstairs.'

He walked quickly around the house, only stopping at one big

window which overlooked the stable lane. He opened the window, carefully looked at the sill with his powerful magnifying lens, and then went upstairs. Mr Holder and I followed him. The rather plain study held only a grey carpet and a large desk.

Holmes went straight to the desk and looked at the lock.

'How was the lock opened?' Holmes asked.

'Just as Arthur had said, the key of the kitchen storage cupboard,' Mr Holder said, picking up a key from the table and handing it over to Holmes.

Holmes took the key and opened the drawer.

'It is a noiseless lock,' he said, 'no wonder it did not wake you.'

He then picked up a black jewel case.

'I think this contains the coronet,' he said, opening the case.

He took out the coronet and placed it on the table. It was a fine specimen of a jeweller's craftsmanship, and the thirty-six stones on the coronet were among the best that I have ever seen. On one side of the coronet was a cracked edge, where a corner holding three gems had been torn away.

'Mr Holder,' Holmes asked. 'This is the corner from which the piece was broken off, is it not? Would you please try to break off another piece?'

Mr Holder withdrew in horror.

'I would not dream of it,' he said.

'Then I will,' Holmes said, and suddenly tried to bend it, using all his strength.

Nothing happened.

'See, I cannot even make a dent, even though I am quite strong,' Holmes said. 'Besides, if it had broken, there would have been a noise like a gunshot! Do you really think all this could have happened that close to your bedroom without you hearing anything?'

'I do not know what to think,' Mr Holder said.

'Hopefully, we can fix that. What do you think, Miss Holder?' Holmes asked.

'I am as confused as my uncle,' Mary replied.

'Your son was not wearing footwear?' Holmes asked Mr Holder.

'No, he was barefoot and in his night clothes,' Mr Holder replied.

'Thank you. Luck seems to be with us, so if we fail, it will only be through our own fault,'

Holmes said, as he headed outside to continue his investigations.

This time, Holmes asked that we stay inside, for he did not want unnecessary footprints to disturb the snow-laden grounds.

He worked, by himself, for more than an hour. Finally, he came in, with wet, snow-covered feet. His face, as usual, was expressionless.

'Thank you, Mr Holder,' he said, 'I will now go back to London. I feel I can be more useful there.'

'But the gems, Mr Holmes, where are they?'

'I cannot say.'

The banker wrung his hands.

'I am never going to see them again!' he cried. 'And my son! Do I dare hope?'

'I still believe he is innocent,' Holmes countered.

'Then what on earth happened last night?' Mr Holder asked, bewildered.

'If you could visit me tomorrow at my Baker Street residence around ten o'clock, I shall be happy to do what I can to make it clearer,' Holmes said. 'Are you sure I can use whatever means to get the stones back?'

'I would give my entire fortune to get them back,' Mr Holder replied.

'Very good. I shall look into the matter. Goodbye,' Holmes said, adding that he might return that evening.

It was obvious that my friend had made up his mind about something, but he refused to tell me anything. We reached our residence at about three o'clock. Holmes disguised himself as a homeless person and left immediately. He returned a few hours later, changed back into his regular clothes and left again.

'I may be late,' he called on his way out, 'I may be very late.'

I waited till about midnight and then retired to my room. It was common for him to disappear for days on end when he was following a lead in an investigation. I do not know when he returned, but he was dressed and having his breakfast when I woke up the next morning.

'Sorry I started without you, Watson,' he said, 'but I am expecting Mr Holder any minute now.'

Just then, Mr Holder came in, looking more miserable than he had the previous morning.

'Two days ago, I was happy, wealthy and well respected. Now I am dishonoured and have no one to comfort me in my old age. First my son, and now, my Mary has run away,' Mr Holder said, hopelessly.

'I think it's my fault. Last night, in my pain, I said that Arthur would have been saved if she had married him. I think I hurt her. Her bed was still made, her room was empty and she has left behind a note.'

The note read:

*Dearest Uncle,*

*I fear that my actions have caused you trouble, and must leave you forever. Do not worry about me. I will be protected and well cared for. Above all, do not search for me, for it will be pointless. I remain, your ever loving,*

*MARY*

'What do you think this means?' Mr Holder asked. 'Is she talking about suicide?'

'Nothing of the kind. In fact, this is probably the best solution. Mr Holder, your troubles are at an end,' Holmes said.

'So you have heard something, Mr Holmes! You have heard something! Where are the gems?' Mr Holder asked.

'You do not think £1,000 each is too much to pay for them?'

'I would pay ten times that amount!' Mr Holder said.

'That would not be unnecessary. Three thousand will cover the matter. And I am guessing you will want to give me a small reward. So, it would cost you £4,000 in total. Have you got your cheque book?'

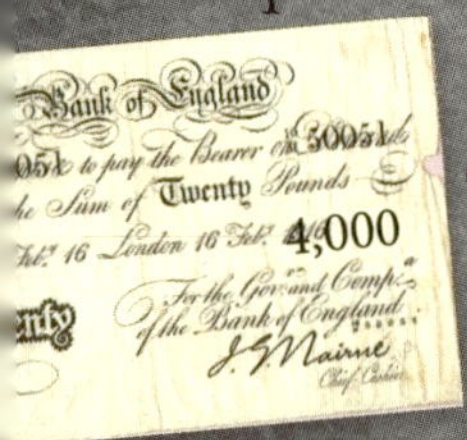


With a dazed look, Mr Holder made out a cheque for £4,000. Holmes walked over to his desk, came back with a little triangular piece of gold with three gems in it and threw it onto the table.

'You have it! I am saved!' Mr Holder exclaimed.

His joy was as intense as his grief. He picked up the piece with a shriek of joy and hugged it to his chest.

'You have one more debt to pay,' Holmes said.

'Name the amount and I will pay it,' Mr Holder said, reaching again for his cheque book.

'No,' said Holmes, 'the debt is not to me. You owe a very humble apology to your poor son, who has acted with great honour throughout this business.'

'Arthur did not take them?' Mr Holder asked.

'I told you that yesterday, and I am saying it again today, Arthur is innocent.'

'Then let us go and tell him the truth as soon as possible.'

'He already knows. I went to meet him as soon as I discovered the truth. I told him what I knew, but he would not talk to me. He might start talking once he hears what you told me this morning.'

'For heaven's sake, explain this amazing mystery!' said Mr Holder.

'Let me start with something that will hurt you: Mary was the culprit. She has run away with Sir George Burnwell, to whom she is engaged.'

'My Mary? That's impossible!' Mr Holder said.

'Unfortunately, that is what actually happened. Neither you nor Arthur knew Sir George Burnwell's true character when you allowed him into your home. He is one of the most dangerous men in England—a ruined gambler, an absolutely desperate villain, a man without a moral sense. It was easy for him to charm her as he had done with hundreds before her. But your niece knows nothing about men like him, and so she let herself believe that she alone had touched his heart,' Holmes said.

'I cannot, and I will not, believe it!' the banker cried.

'Let me, then, explain what happened at your house last night,' Holmes said.

'When she thought you had gone to bed, Mary slipped down and talked to her lover through the window overlooking the stable lane. I found his footsteps in the snow outside. She told him about the coronet. His wicked greed sparked; the villain then convinced her to steal the coronet,' Holmes told Mr Holder.

'She had just returned after speaking to him when she saw you coming down the stairs. She then quickly shut the window and told you about the maid's meeting with her wooden-legged lover, which was perfectly true. I found

their footprints in the snow near the gate as well. The deep toe and light heel marks showed that the woman had run back to the house,' Holmes continued.

'Arthur went to bed after he spoke with you, but could not sleep because he was worried about his unpaid debt. In the middle of the night, he heard someone walking past his door.

'Arthur looked out of his door and saw Mary entering your study. The astonished boy then waited in the dark to see what happened. When Mary came out of the study, Arthur saw, in the semi-darkness, that she was carrying the crown. When she went downstairs, he followed her and hid behind a curtain, to see what would happen. He saw her open the window secretly, hand the coronet to someone outside, close the window again, and then sneak back into her own room.

'He realized what a blow the theft would be to you, and so decided to get it back. But since he did not want to expose the woman he loved, he waited for her to return to her room. Arthur opened the window and, without waiting to put on any footwear, rushed out into the snow. He saw a man—Sir George Burnwell—in the distance and chased him.'

'Sir George tried to escape but Arthur caught him. The two struggled over the coronet. Suddenly, there was a loud crack, and Arthur found himself holding the twisted crown. It had snapped under the combined strength of the two men. Arthur then rushed back and closed the window. He had just realized that the coronet was twisted and was trying to straighten it when you found him.'

'You then accused him of stealing the coronet, instead of thanking him for his effort. This angered him. However, he could not explain the situation without revealing the role that Mary—the woman he loved—had played,' Holmes said.

'That is why she fainted when she saw the coronet!' Mr Holder said, as realization came into his mind. 'And that's also why he wanted to go out before I had him arrested! He wanted to see if he could find the missing piece. How cruel I have been!'

Holmes continued, 'When I looked around yesterday, I found two sets of footprints in the stable lane. One pair belonged to someone who had been wearing boots, while the other set belonged to a barefoot man—your son, Arthur. Boots had walked in both directions, but the barefoot man had run quickly. I followed the footprints to where the scuffle had occurred.

'Then, I examined the window inside the house and found that someone had passed through it with wet feet. This was a vital clue, but I was still unsure who the culprit was. It had to be your niece or the maids, but who would Arthur want to protect?

'Then, I remembered that you said Arthur loved Mary, and that you had seen her at the window. You had also said she fainted when she saw the coronet. This convinced me that Arthur had lied to protect Mary.'

'Her companion was the next piece of the puzzle. You have a limited social circle but that circle included Sir George Burnwell, a known rake. He must have been the one in the boots, who had taken the missing gems.'

'In the evening, I disguised myself and went to Sir George's house. There, I bribed his valet, and bought a pair of Sir George's used boots. I then took the boots back to Streatham and checked them against the prints in the snow. They matched perfectly.

'Later, I came home, changed my clothes and went out to meet Sir George. At first, he denied everything. But when I offered to buy the gems at £1,000 each, he said, "That cheat! He only gave me £600 for all three!" I soon managed to learn the name of the man who had bought the beryls, tracked him down and bought them back at £1,000 each. Thereafter, I went to see Arthur and finally came home.'

'You have saved England from certain scandal,' Mr Holder said, rising from his chair. 'Thank you! Thank you, Mr Holmes. But I am still upset about Mary. Where on earth could she be?'

'Wherever she is, she is with Sir George Burnwell, and they will soon be punished for their crimes,' Holmes said, showing Mr Holder out.

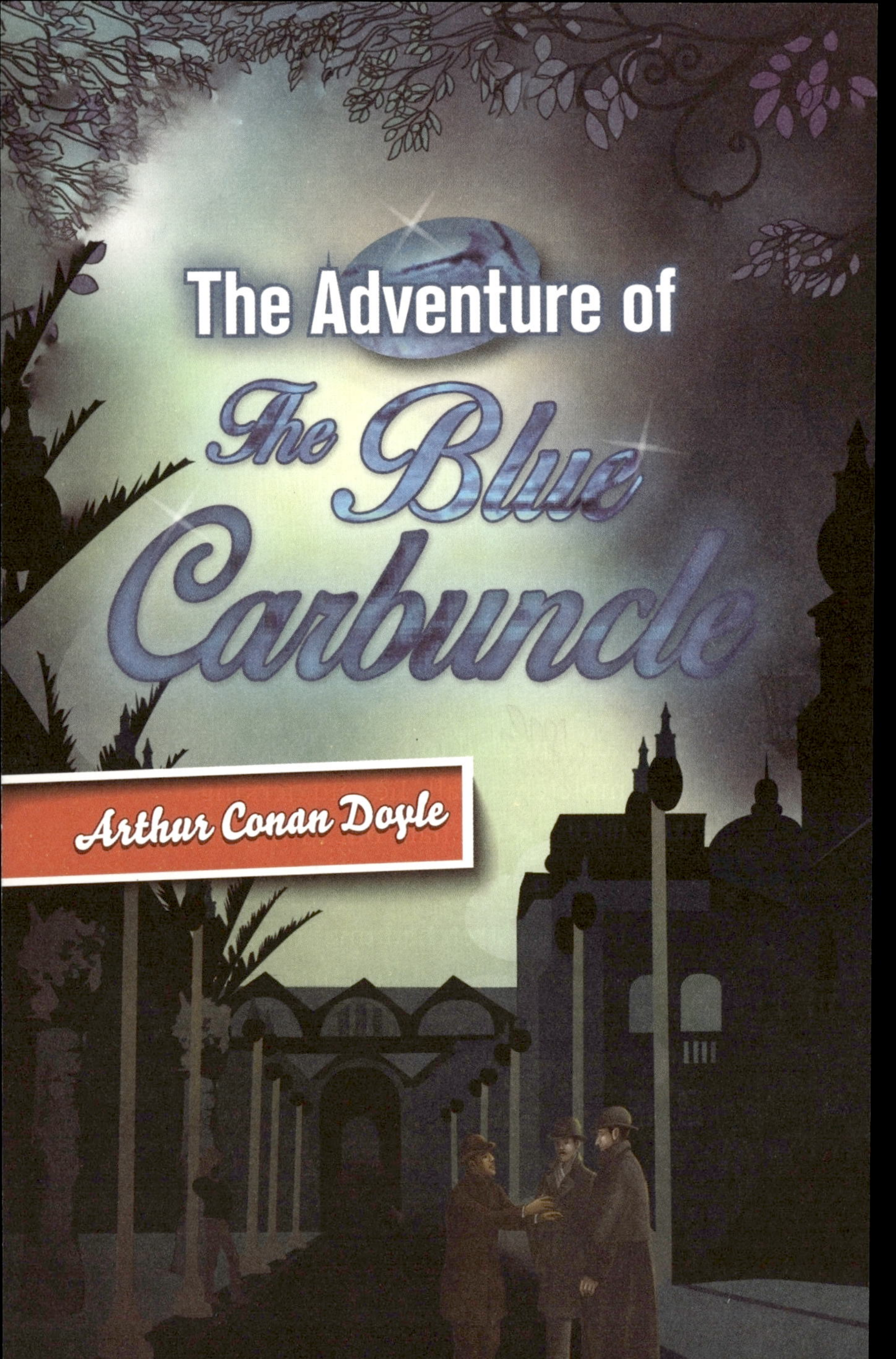
The Adventure of
The Blue Carbuncle
Arthur Conan Doyle

It was the second day after Christmas, and I had gone over to Baker Street to wish my friend Sherlock Holmes compliments of the season. Holmes was relaxing on the sofa in a purple dressing gown. At arm's length, lay a pile of crumpled newspapers. He had evidently just finished reading them. On the chair next to him, were a worn out felt hat, a pair of forceps and a magnifying glass, suggesting that Holmes had been looking at the hat.

'You seem busy,' I said, 'I hope I'm not interrupting.'

Holmes looked up.

'Not at all! I'm glad to have a friend to discuss this. It's completely small,' he said, jerking a thumb towards the old hat, 'but I find one or two points about it quite interesting.'

I sat down and stretched my fingers, stiff with the cold, towards the crackling fire.

'I suppose it is not as innocent as it looks,' I said, 'that old hat is some clue in a deadly crime.'

'No,' Holmes said, 'no crime. Just one of those strange incidents you get when you have four million people pushing with each other in the space of a few square miles. Occasionally, interesting

events do occur that are not criminal in nature, as you already know.'

'Yes,' I said, 'of your last six cases, three had nothing to do with any sort of legal crime.'

'Definitely,' Holmes replied, 'I expect this to fall into the same innocent category. Do you remember Peterson, the Police Commissioner?'

'Yes,' I said, 'Is that his hat?'

'No, but he found it. He brought it to me on Christmas morning, along with a fat goose that—I'm sure—is being cooked in the Peterson kitchen as we speak.'

'Look at it, Watson,' Holmes went on, 'not as any old hat, but as an intellectual problem. Here are the facts: Around four o'clock on Christmas morning, Peterson was returning home after some fun, when he saw ahead of him, a tallish man in a hat, walking with a slight stagger, and carrying a white goose over his shoulder. A while later, this stranger got into a fight with a little group of ruffians. They knocked down his hat and the man raised his stick to protect himself but ended up breaking the shop window behind him. Peterson tried to help the man. But he was shocked at having broken the window. Seeing an official in uniform coming towards him, he panicked, dropped his bird and ran away. The ruffians also ran away when they saw Peterson, so he got back the hat and goose and came to see me.'

'Why didn't he give them back to their owner?' I asked.

'I was coming to that,' Holmes replied. 'While the bird had a tag saying, "for Mrs Henry Baker", and the hat is marked "HB", there are hundreds of Henry Bakers in London, making it very difficult to find the owner.'

'Anyway, we kept the goose till this morning, when there were signs that, despite the frost, it would not keep fresh much longer. So Peterson took it away, while I continue to retain the hat of the stranger who lost his Christmas dinner.'

'Has he advertised?' I asked.

'No,' Holmes replied.

'Then how will you identify him?'

'I have his hat. Here is my lens. You know my methods. See what you can deduce about the hat's owner.'

I took the hat in my hands and turned it over. It was a very ordinary black hard-felt hat, rather

worse for wear, with a dull silk lining that had once been red. I did not see a maker's name but, as Holmes had pointed out, there were the initials 'HB' The brim was pierced for a hat securer, but the elastic was missing. Apart from this, it was very dusty, and spotted in several places, although there seemed to be some attempt to hide the stains by smearing them with ink.

'I can see nothing,' I said, returning the hat to Holmes.

'On the contrary, Watson,' Holmes said, 'you can see everything. You can't, however, use what you see to draw conclusions.'

'Then tell me what I have to infer,' I replied.

'It is obvious that the man is an intellectual, fairly well-to-do until about three years ago,' Holmes said.

'He formerly had a great deal of foresight, but not anymore. He has also been on a moral decline. Judging from that and the fall in his fortunes, he has probably taken to drinking in the past three years and, finally, he has probably lost the love of his wife', Holmes continued.

'My dear Holmes!' I interrupted.

'He has, however, had some amount of self-respect,' Holmes went on, ignoring my interruption. 'He rarely goes out, and is physically unfit. He is middle-aged, has had a haircut recently and he applies lime cream on his hair.'

'Certainly, you are joking, Holmes!'

'Not in the least. Can you still not see how I came to these conclusions?' he asked.

'No,' I replied, feeling a little stupid. 'How did you deduce that the man is an intellectual?'

In answer, Holmes put the hat on. It fell down his forehead and settled on the bridge of his nose.

'With such a large head, he must surely have something in it!' Holmes explained.

He went on, 'As to his fall in fortune, this style of hat—with the slight curl to the brim—was in fashion about three years ago. Look at the excellent lining. It is a hat of the very best quality. If a man could afford this hat three years ago, and has not bought another one since then, surely his fortunes have fallen.'

'That is clear enough now,' I said. 'What about the foresight and moral decline?'

Holmes laughed. He put his finger on the little disc and loop of the hat securer.

'Here is the foresight. Hat securers have to be ordered. That he went to such lengths shows he had a certain amount of foresight. However, he has not replaced the broken elastic, showing a drop in foresight. This is turn shows a moral weakening. The fact he has tried to hide some of these stains shows he has some self-respect left.'

'As to the rest, there are a number of very short hair-ends caught in the lining, showing he recently visited a barber. The smell of lime-cream is clear and the dust on the hat is brown house dust, rather than the gritty grey dust of the street. Moreover, the moisture stains show that the man sweat freely and was not in the best of physical shape.'

'But, you said his wife has stopped loving him.'

'His hat has not been brushed in weeks. No loving wife lets her husband leave the house like that.'

'He might be a bachelor,' I tried.

'Ah! You forget the band on the goose's leg. It was a gift to his wife, a peace offering, unless I am mistaken.'

'That's very creative, but as you said, no crime was committed, so this seems like a waste of energy,' I said.

Holmes opened his mouth to answer, but the door flew open and Peterson, the commissioner, rushed in with shining cheeks and a look of amazement on his face.

'Sir! Look what my wife found in the crop of the goose!' he called, holding up a brilliant blue gemstone.

It was slightly smaller than the size of a bean, but so pure that it twinkled in his hand.

'By Jove, Peterson! Do you know what you are holding?'

'A precious stone? A diamond, sir?' he asked, 'It cuts into glass as if it were putty.'

'Not a precious stone,' Holmes said. 'The precious stone!'

'Not the Countess of Morcar's blue carbuncle!' I exclaimed.

'Precisely that!' Holmes said. '*The Times* has been carrying advertisements about it every day for the past five days. The countess is offering a

£1,000 reward for it, but its value is at least twenty times that amount; not counting the feelings the countess attaches to it.'

'A thousand pounds!' Peterson exclaimed, falling into a chair and staring at us in turns.

'Wasn't the blue carbuncle stolen from the Hotel Cosmopolitan?' I asked.

'Definitely, on 22 December, just five days ago. John Horner, a plumber, was accused of removing it from the lady's jewel case. The proof against him was so strong he was arrested immediately. I believe I have the newspaper report somewhere here,' Sherlock said, searching through his crumpled papers.

He finally found what he was looking for, smoothened out the paper and read the following report: 'John Horner, 26, plumber, was charged with stealing the valuable gem known as the blue carbuncle from the jewel case of the Countess of Morcar on 22 December. According to witness James Ryder, an attendant at the hotel, he had shown Horner up to the Countess's dressing room on the day of the robbery to solder the second bar of the grate, which was loose. He had remained with Horner until he was called away.'

The report continued:

'By the time he returned, Ryder said, Horner had disappeared. The cupboard had been forced open, and the Countess's jewel case lay empty on the dressing table. Ryder raised an alarm, and Horner was arrested the same evening; but the stone was not discovered. Catherine Cusack, maid to the Countess, said that on hearing Ryder's shout, she rushed to the room and found it as Ryder described. Inspector Bradstreet, who arrested Horner, said the latter struggled crazily, and protested his innocence in the strongest terms. Since the accused has previously been framed for robbery, the case was brought before the criminal court. Horner, who had shown signs of intense emotion during the proceedings, fainted away at the conclusion and was carried out of court.'

'So much for the court,' said Holmes thoughtfully. 'What we need to do now is solve the sequence of events from a robbed jewel case at one end to the crop of a goose at the other end. See, Watson, our findings weren't a wasted effort, after all. Here is the stone. The stone came from the goose, and the goose came from Mr Henry Baker, the gentleman with the hat. So we now need to find Mr Baker and uncover his role in this mystery. The simplest way to do this, I feel, is to advertise in the evening papers.'

Holmes then took hold of a pen and paper and wrote: 'Found at the corner of Goodge Street, a goose and a black felt hat. Mr Henry Baker can have the same by visiting 221B, Baker Street, at 6:30 this evening.'

Holmes wanted to publish the above notice in the lost and found section of the local daily.

'That is clear and short,' I said, 'but will he see it?'

'He is sure to be keeping an eye on the papers,' Holmes said, 'since the loss is a heavy one to a poor man. He was so scared about breaking the window that when he saw Peterson, all he could think of was running. However, since then, he must have bitterly regretted his impulse to drop the bird. Plus, his name will draw his attention. Even if he does not see it, one of his acquaintances might and point him to it. Peterson, run down to the advertising agency and have this fit into the papers.'

'Which ones, sir?' Peterson asked.

'All of them,' Holmes said.

'And the stone, sir?' Peterson asked.

'I will keep the stone, thank you,' Holmes said, adding, 'And Peterson, could you buy a goose and drop it off here on your way home, so I can give it to Mr Baker in place of the bird your family is now eating.'

221 B

After Peterson left, Holmes pointed out the little blue gem and said, 'I'll drop this into my safe and drop the Countess a line saying we have it.'

'So, do you think this Mr Baker would know anything about it?' I asked.

'It is more likely that he had no idea that the bird he was carrying was actually worth more than its weight in gold. But I cannot know for sure until I speak to him this evening.'

'Can you do nothing till then?' I asked.

'Absolutely nothing,' Sherlock said.

'In that case, I'll be back in the evening. I would really like to see how this turns out,' I said as I left.

When I returned to Baker Street, a little after 6:30 in the evening, a tall man in a Scotch bonnet and a buttoned-up coat was waiting outside. Just as I reached 221B, the door opened and Sherlock let the man in.

As I had expected, the man was Mr Henry Baker.

'Good evening,' said Holmes, offering him the chair by the fire. 'Is that your hat?'

'Yes sir, undoubtedly,' Mr Baker said.

He was a large man with rounded shoulders, a big head and a broad, intelligent face, sloping down to a pointed beard of greying brown. A touch of red in nose and cheeks, with a slight shake of his extended hand, reminded me of Sherlock's initial judgement of the man.

His black coat was buttoned up to his chin in front, with the collar turned up. His lank wrists protruded from his sleeves without any sign of a cuff or a shirt. He spoke in a slow staccato, choosing his words with care, and generally gave the impression of a man of learning, who had recently seen a slide in fortune.

'We have had your belongings for a few days now,' Holmes said. 'We had expected you to advertise, giving your address. Why did you not?'

Our visitor gave a sorry laugh.

'Money is not as plentiful with me as it once was,' he remarked. 'I was convinced that the thugs who attacked me had taken both my hat and the bird. I did not want to waste any more money on what I felt as a hopeless cause.'

'Naturally,' Holmes said. 'By the way, that goose ... we had to eat it.'

'Eat it!' Our visitor half rose in his excitement.

'Yes. It would not have been any good to anyone if we hadn't. However, I am hoping that the other goose—the one on that sideboard—would make up for the one you lost. It is about the same weight and perfectly fresh,' Holmes said.

'Certainly!' Mr Baker answered with a sigh of relief.

'Of course, we still have the feathers, legs, crop and so on of your own bird, so if you wish—'

'They might make tokens of my adventure, but beyond that, what could I possibly do with them?' he asked, giving a hearty laugh. 'No sir, with your permission, I will confine myself to the excellent bird I see on the sideboard.'

Sherlock looked sharply at me with a slight shrug of his shoulders.

'Here's your hat, then, and bird,' Sherlock said, handing Mr Baker the objects.

'By the way,' he added, 'would you mind telling where you got that bird?'

'Certainly,' he replied, putting in the goose firmly under his arm, 'Windigate, the host of the Alpha Inn, which I frequent, set up a goose club. I paid a few pence each week, and got a goose at Christmas. And, well, you know the rest of the story.'

'So much for Mr Henry Baker,' Holmes said, as Mr Henry Baker shut the door behind him. 'He knows nothing at all about the matter. If you are not too hungry, could we delay dinner and follow up on this tip while it is still hot?'

I wasn't very hungry and so we decided to go and find Windigate of the Alpha Inn. It was a bitterly cold night, so we covered ourselves up and headed out. The stars were shining coldly in a cloudless sky, and our breath fogged up like smoke. Our footfalls rang out sharply and loudly as we swung through Wimpole Street, Harley Street, and then through Wigmore Street into Oxford Street.

In about fifteen minutes, we had reached the Alpha Inn in Bloomsbury. Holmes walked in and ordered two beers from a ruddy-faced, white-aproned landlord.

'Your beer would be excellent if it is as good as your geese,' Sherlock said.

The landlord was surprised.

'My geese!'

'Yes. I was speaking to Mr Henry Baker about half an hour ago. He was part of your goose club.'

'Ah! Yes. But, you see, those aren't our geese. I bought two dozen geese from a salesman in Covent Garden,' Windigate said.

'Indeed!' Sherlock said, 'I know some of them. Which was it?'

'Breckinridge,' Windigate replied.

So we thanked the landlord and set off to look for Breckinridge.

'Remember Watson, that even though we have a humble goose at one end of the mystery, at the other, we have a man who will certainly go to jail for seven years unless we prove his innocence. It is possible that we might prove his guilt but, in any case, we are following a line of investigation that the police had missed, thanks to a lucky coincidence,' Sherlock said.

We passed across Holborn, down Endell Street and through a zigzag of slums to Covent Garden Market. One of the largest stalls bore the name of Breckinridge. The proprietor, a horsy-looking man, with a sharp face and trim side-whiskers, was helping a boy to put up the shutters.

'Good evening. It's a cold night,' Holmes said.

The salesman nodded and shot a questioning look at my companion.

'Sold out of geese, I see,' Holmes continued, pointing at the bare slabs of marble.

'You can get 500 tomorrow morning,' Breckinridge said.

'That's no good,' Sherlock said.

'Well, there are some there,' the man said, pointing to a nearby stall.

'But I was put forward to you.'

'By whom?'

'The landlord at the Alpha Inn.'

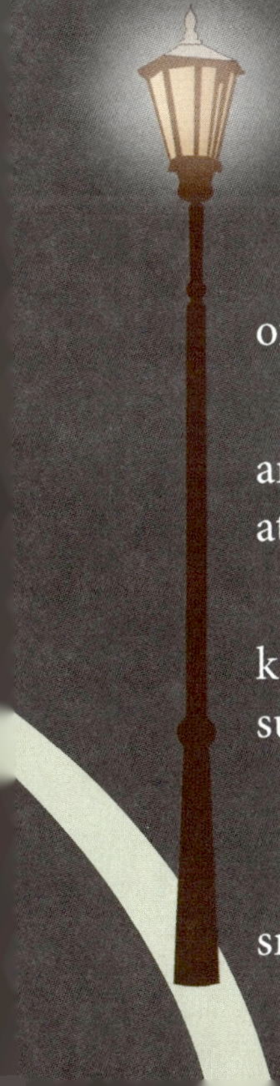

'Oh yes, I sent him two dozen.'

'Fine bird, they were, too. Now, where did you get them from?'

To my surprise, the question sparked off a burst of anger from the salesman.

'Now, then, mister,' he said, head cocked and his arms crossed, 'what are you driving at? Tell me straight.'

'It is straight enough. I would like to know who sold you the geese which you supplied to the Alpha,' Sherlock replied.

'Well,' the man said, 'I won't tell you.'

'There's no need to get warm over such a small thing.'

'Warm! You'd be warm too, if you've been annoyed as much as I have. Why should anyone bother me about something I have paid good money for? "Where are the geese?" and "Who did you sell the geese to?" and "What will you take for the geese?" One would think these were the only geese in the world!'

He would have gone on if Holmes had not interrupted him.

'I have no connection with anyone else looking for the birds,' Sherlock said carelessly, 'if you don't tell me, the bet is off. I have a fiver that those geese were bred in the countryside.'

'Well then,' snapped the salesman, 'you've lost your fiver. They are town bred.'

'I'll never believe that!' Sherlock said.

'Would you care to bet?' Breckinridge asked.

'I would simply be taking your money, for I am sure I am right. But, ok, I'll play along,' Sherlock said, and bet a sovereign.

Breckinridge called his assistant and told him to bring the books.

'Here, Mr Smartypants, is proof that they are town bred,' the salesman enjoyed greatly, and showed us an entry into his books.

The first column said, 'Mrs Oakshott, 117, Brixton Road, egg and poultry supplier', the next said 'December 22, twenty-four geese at 7s. 6d. The third column said, 'sold to Mr Windigate, the Alpha, at 12s.'

'What do you say now?' Breckinridge asked, smugly.

Holmes looked irritated, admitted defeat and paid the man and left. We hadn't gone much further when Holmes burst out laughing. He explained that he had seen a betting slip in the man's pocket.

'Without the bet, he would not have given me this much information, even if I had paid him £100,' he said.

We were trying to decide whether to visit Mrs Oakshott that night, or the next day, when we were disturbed by a fuss taking place back at Breckinridge's stall.

The salesman was shaking his fist and yelling at a little rat-faced fellow, 'I've had enough of you and your geese! If you come back here, I'll set the dog on you. Bring Mrs Oakshott here and I'll answer her, but what have you go to do with it? Did I buy the geese off you?'

'No,' Ratface whined, 'but one of them was mine still.'

'Go ask Mrs Oakshott for it then,' came the retort.

'But she told me to ask you.'

'I don't care if you ask the King of Prussia. I've had enough of you! Get out!' the salesman shouted and rushed at the little man, who fled into the darkness.

'Ha!' whispered Holmes. 'This might save us a trip to Brixton. Come with me, and we shall see what this fellow knows.

Marching forward, we soon overtook the little

man and Sherlock touched him on the shoulder. He turned around, and I saw that his face was pale.

'Who are you?' he asked. 'What do you want?'

'Excuse me, I overheard your questions and feel we could be of help,' Holmes said.

'How can you possibly know anything about it?' the man asked, suspiciously.

'My name is Sherlock Holmes and it is my business to know what other people don't know. I know you are looking for some geese that Mrs Oakshott sold to Breckinridge, who then sold it

to Mr Windigate of the Alpha and by him, to his club, of which Mr Henry Baker is a member.'

'Oh, sir! Then you are the very man I needed to meet. You have no idea how interested I am in that goose!' the little man cried.

'In that case, we should continue this discussion in my cosy room,' Sherlock said, calling a passing taxi. 'But, please, tell me, what is your name?'

The man paused for a second before answering.

'John Robinson.'

'Your real name,' Sherlock said sweetly. 'It is always hard to remember an alias.'

The man turned red.

He said, 'My real name is James Ryder.'

'And you are the head attendant at the Hotel Cosmopolitan. Please step into the carriage, and I shall tell you everything you might want to know,' Holmes said.

Ryder looked unsure as to what to expect. Then he stepped into the horse carriage and in half an hour, we were back at Holmes's residence. Ryder sat in a chair near the fire.

When we got there, Holmes surprised Ryder by disclosing that he was interested in just one bird—white, with a black bar on its tail.

'Can you tell me where it is?' Ryder asked.

'It came here,' Sherlock said, 'and I can see why you are so interested in it. After it was dead, it laid an egg—the brightest blue egg I have ever seen. I have it here in my museum.'

Ryder stood up, nervously holding the mantelpiece. When Holmes took out the gem, Ryder seemed undecided whether to claim it or deny any knowledge of its existence.

'Game's up, Ryder,' Holmes said quietly. 'Hold still, man, or you'll fall into the fireplace.'

Ryder had walked unsteadily for a minute, so I helped him into a chair and gave him a spot of brandy to steady his nerves.

'He's too weak to do a crime with any authority,' Holmes noted.

'I have almost all the pieces of the puzzle. Tell me, Ryder, how did you hear of the Countess of Morcar's little stone?

'Catherine Cusack told me,' Ryder answered.

'Aah! Her ladyship's maid. Well, better men than you have surrendered to the urge of earning sudden wealth easily. However, you were devious in executing the plan. You knew that Horner, the plumber, had already been caught in a similar trouble, so you came up a set-up, letting him take

the blame for your crime. What did you do then?' Holmes asked.

He then answered his own question, 'Your partner Cusack then created a problem in the Countess's rooms and you made sure that Horner was sent to fix it. Then, when he had left, you robbed the jewellery case, stole the stone, raised the alarm and had the unfortunate man arrested.'

Here, Ryder threw himself onto the floor, begging for mercy. He said he had never committed a crime before and would never do so again. He then asked that Holmes not take the matter to court.

'It is very well to cringe and cry, but an innocent man is waiting for trial because of you,' Holmes said sternly.

'I will flee the country, sir,' Ryder cried, 'they can't find him guilty if I don't testify against him.'

'We will discuss that later. Now

tell us how the stone got inside the goose to start with,' Holmes said.

Ryder then told us the whole story. After he had stolen the gemstone, he realized he had to hide it.

Ryder went into hiding on the goose farm that his sister, Mrs Oakshott, ran. Mrs Oakshott had promised to give him a goose for Christmas. So while he was there, he caught a goose, and forced it to swallow the gem. The bird made a scary noise, which Mrs Oakshott came out to investigate. When Ryder saw his sister, he

panicked and let the bird go. She asked what he was doing among the birds, and he said that he was deciding which one he wanted. His sister pointed out to a large all-white bird and said that she had been fattening that one up especially for him. But Ryder insisted that he wanted the one with the black bar on its tail, even though it was smaller. They argued, but actually Ryder picked up the bird with a black bar on its tail and took it home.

When he cut it open, the stone was not there. So he ran back to Mrs Oakshoot and asked if there was another goose with a similar black bar on its tail.

'She said there was, and that they were identical,' Ryder said. 'She also said that the others had all been sold. I have been following the blasted birds since then.'

By this time, Ryder was on the floor, a sobbing mess.

'Please don't call the police, sir,' he begged. 'I will flee. I will not appear in court to give evidence.'

'Get out! And always remember that I am watching you!' Holmes said.

When Ryder had left, I asked Holmes why he had let the man go.

'If he does not appear in court, there is no evidence against Horner. Besides, we cannot do the police's job for them. Anyway, enough of this. Let us have dinner.'

And, so, we finally sat down to eat.

The Boscombe Valley Mystery
Arthur Conan Doyle

During breakfast one morning, I received a telegram from Sherlock Holmes. It said he had been invited to consult on the Boscombe Valley tragedy and was leaving on the 11:15 train. He asked if I would travel with him for a few days.

My experience of serving in Afghanistan taught me to be a prompt and ready traveller, and I was soon at the railway station. Holmes was pacing up and down the platform, his tall thin figure made even thinner and taller by his long grey travelling-cloak and close-fitting cloth cap.

'I am glad you could come,' Holmes said. 'It is good to have someone who is completely reliable. The local authorities are usually either worthless or biased.'

We had a compartment to ourselves. For a while, Holmes took notes as he read the large pile of newspapers he had brought along. Suddenly, he rolled them all into a ball and tossed them aside.

'Do you know anything about the case?' he asked.

'No, I haven't read the newspapers for a few days.'

'I have just read all the recent ones to gather the facts but the London papers haven't been very in-depth. This seems to be one of those seemingly simple cases which turn out to be extremely difficult. Oddities can be valuable clues, but seemingly commonplace crimes are the most difficult to solve. In this one, however, the police have established a strong case against the murdered man's son.'

'It was murder, then?' I asked.

'Apparently, but I cannot be sure until I have investigated it myself.'

He then started to explain what he had obtained from the press: 'Mr John Turner owns the largest piece in Boscombe Valley, a country district near Ross, in Herefordshire. He returned to England a few years ago after making a fortune in Australia.

'He rented out one of his farms—Hatherley—to Mr Charles McCarthy, who he had known in Australia. Although Mr McCarthy was Mr Turner's tenant, they behaved as equals, and were frequently seen together. Mr McCarthy has an eighteen-year-old son, and Mr Turner, a daughter of the same age, Alice Turner. Both men were widowers and led quiet lives, avoiding the company of English neighbours. Mr McCarthy had two servants while Mr Turner had at least six.

'While in Ross last Monday morning, Mr McCarthy told his man servant that he had important appointment at three o'clock at the Boscombe Pool—a small lake about a quarter mile from his house. He never came back from that meeting.

'Two witnesses—an unknown old woman and William Crowder, one of Mr Turner's gamekeepers—said they saw Mr McCarthy walking towards the Boscombe Pool that afternoon. Soon after, he saw McCarthy's son, Mr James McCarthy, pass the same way with a gun under his arm.

'Crowder believes the son was following his father. He did not give that any importance until he heard about the tragedy that evening.

'A third witness—Patience Moran, the fourteen-year-old daughter of Mr McCarthy's lodge keeper—said she saw Mr McCarthy and his son in the grass and reeds that surround the thick woods surrounding the lake.

'Miss Moran had been picking flowers when she saw the men. The father was shouting at his son and the son raised his hand as if to strike his father. This violence frightened her so much that she ran to tell her mother what she had seen. She hardly finished her account, when the younger Mr McCarthy came in running, to say he had found his father dead in the woods, and to ask for Moran's help. He was very upset, without his gun or his hat, and his right hand and sleeve were stained with fresh blood.

'The lodge keeper went along with Mr James McCarthy to the corpse, which was stretched out upon the grass beside the pool. The head had been bashed in with a heavy blunt object, quite possibly the base of his son's gun, which was found in the grass near the body.

'The young man was arrested, charged with murder and presented before the criminal court,' Holmes concluded.

'I could hardly imagine a more critical case,' I remarked.

'Circumstantial proof is a very tricky thing,' Holmes went on, thoughtfully. 'It may seem to indicate one thing, but if you shift your own point of view, you may find that it indicates quite another thing entirely. I must admit that the case against the young man looks exceedingly strong. He could very well be guilty, but many people—including Miss Turner—do not believe that. They hired Mr Lestrade to prove his innocence. A rather puzzled Mr Lestrade then referred the case to me.'

'I am afraid,' I said, 'that the facts are so obvious that you will find little credit to be gained from this case.'

'Nothing is more misleading than obvious fact,' Holmes answered, laughingly. 'Besides, we might discover something that Mr Lestrade missed. Anyway, the newspaper reports reveal one or two interesting points.'

'What are they?'

'One, the arrest did not take place until Mr James McCarthy returned to Hatherley Farm. Two, the accused said that he was not surprised when the constable placed him under arrest, and that he deserved it. But then he followed it with a statement of innocence.'

'How suspicious!' I said.

'Just the opposite,' Holmes said. 'However innocent, James McCarthy must have realized the amount of trouble he was in, and a tricky man might have acted surprised or angry, even though these are not natural responses to such situations.

His reaction marks him as an innocent man or one of considerable self-restraint.'

'As to his remark about his just desserts,' Holmes continued, 'the lad had fought with his father, just before he was found dead. His remark shows regret rather than guilt.'

'What did the young man say of the matter?'

'Read it yourself,' Holmes said, handing a copy of the local Herefordshire paper that carried the unlucky young man's statement. The report quoted the younger Mr McCarthy. It said: 'I was at Bristol for three days, and returned on Monday morning. My father was not home when I arrived, and the maid said he was in Ross with the groom. I later heard his carriage in the yard. I looked out of my window and saw him get out and walk rapidly out of the yard. However, I did not know where he was going. I then took my gun and went out in the direction of the Boscombe Pool, intending to shoot some rabbits.'

'On my way,' the report continued, 'I saw William Crowder, the game-keeper, as he has already stated; but I was not following my father. About a hundred yards from the pool I heard a cry of "Cooee!" which was a usual signal between my father and me. I then hurried forward, and found him standing by the pool. He seemed very surprised to see me and demanded to know why

I was there. We then got into an argument, which almost led to blows, for my father had a violent temper. Realizing that his anger was getting out of control, I left him and turned towards Hatherley Farm. I had not gone very far when I heard a terrible choas behind me, so I turned and ran back to find my father's head bashed in. I dropped my gun and held him in my arms. He died soon after, but before he died, he said something that sounded like "rat".

'I then went to Moran's house to ask for assistance since it was nearby. I have no idea who attacked my father. He was not a popular man, but did not have any active enemies as far as I know.'

The report said the accused had refused to disclose the subject of his final quarrel with his father. It also said that when questioned, he said he did not know why his father would signal to him when he was not even aware he had returned from Bristol.

The report continued, 'Asked if he had seen anything suspicious, Mr James McCarthy said he could not be certain, but that he may have seen a grey piece of cloth lying on the ground when he rushed to his father's side. When he went to look for it later, it was gone, he said.'

The report also pointed out that James McCarthy could not explain how the cloth had been moved while he had been so close.

'They do have a point,' I said.

Holmes laughed, 'Are you saying this young man has too much imagination, or too little? If he has too much, why did he not invent a cause for the quarrel which would gain him public sympathy? If he has too little, how did he make up the rat reference, and the vanishing cloth? For now, I will assume that this young man is not lying.'

We soon reached Ross, where a lean ferret-like man, secretly and sly, was waiting for us. I recognized Lestrade, of Scotland Yard, immediately. Lestrade then drove us to the Hereford Arms, where he had booked us a room.

'I'm sure you are in a hurry to get to the crime scene,' Lestrade said, 'so I have booked you a carriage.'

'That is very nice of you,' Holmes replied, lighting a pipe, 'but the weather is nice, and this sofa is very comfortable. I doubt I use the carriage tonight.'

Lestrade laughed indulgently.

'No doubt you have seen from the newspaper reports

that this is a simple case. However, one cannot refuse a lady and she wants your opinion.'

Lestrade had hardly finished speaking when a lovely young woman—Miss Turner—rushed in. Her violet eyes shining, a pink shine upon her cheeks, she has lost her natural reserve in her overpowering concern.

Miss Turner looked quickly at both of us and quickly, and correctly, addressed my companion.

'Mr Sherlock Holmes!' she cried, 'I am so glad that you have come. I have come to tell you that James didn't do it. The charge against him is absurd. I have known him since we were little, and I know he is too gentle to hurt a fly.'

'I will do my best to clear him,' Holmes said.

'You have read the reports. Do you not think that he is innocent?'

'He may be.'

Miss Turner looked boldly at Lestrade, and he shrugged.

'I am afraid my colleague has jumped to conclusions,' he said.

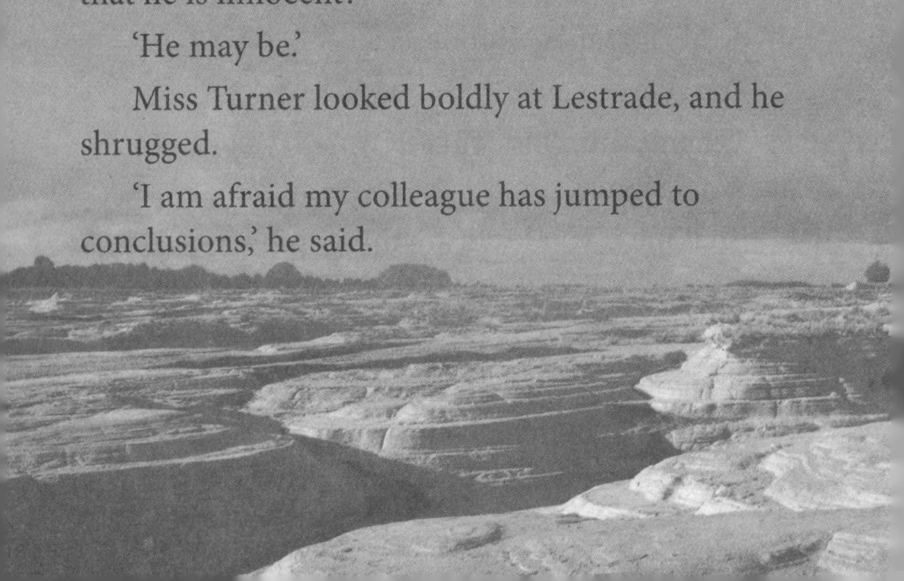

'But he's right! And I know why James did not want to talk about the quarrel with his father—it was about me,' Miss Turner said.

She explained, 'Mr McCarthy had wanted James to marry me, but our friendship has always been pure. They quarrelled often, and I am sure this was one of those fights.'

'Did your father want this union?' Holmes asked.

'No, just Mr McCarthy.'

'Thank you,' Holmes said. 'May I call on your father tomorrow?'

'I am afraid the doctor won't allow it. Poor father has never been strong, but he had a nervous breakdown after Mr McCarthy's murder. Mr McCarthy was the only man who had known Dad in the old days in Victoria.'

'The gold mines in Victoria, where Mr Turner made his fortune?' Holmes asked.

'Yes, certainly.'

'Thank you, Miss Turner. You have been of great assistance.'

'Tell me if you learn anything tomorrow. No doubt, you will visit James. And when you do, Mr Holmes, please tell him I know he is innocent.'

'I will, Miss Turner.'

'I must go home now for Dad is very ill. Goodbye and good luck,' she said, rushing out.

We soon heard her carriage leaving.

'Holmes, that was cruel,' Lestrade said after a few minutes' silence.

'Why would you give her hope when you know you are going to disappoint her?'

'I think I know how to clear James McCarthy,' Holmes said. 'Do you have an order to see him in prison?'

'Yes, but only for you and me.'

'I've changed my mind. Do we have time to see him tonight?'

'Yes,' Lestrade said, and they left, leaving me to my own devices.

I thought my medical training would help me learn something more from the nature of the injuries and so reread the newspaper report. The posterior third of the left parietal bone and the left half of the occipital bone had been shattered. I

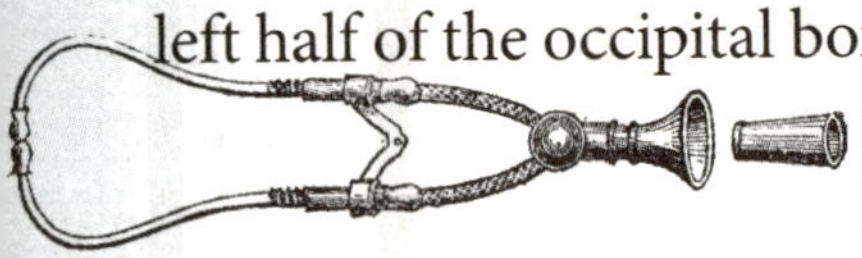

felt the spot on my own head. That area could only be struck from behind. Why would James McCarthy hit his father on the back of his head when he had been facing him during the argument? The man may have turned around before the blow fell, but this information might be important.

There was also the strange reference to the rat. It could not be madness, since that is not usual in a man dying from a sudden blow.

Also, if the young man was telling the truth, the mysterious grey cloth—possibly maybe a coat—might have been dropped by the murderer, who had then gone and retrieved it when the boy went for help. I had a feeling Holmes would soon prove young McCarthy's innocence.

Holmes returned, alone, since Lestrade was staying in town.

'We shall visit the pool tomorrow morning when we are not so tired from our long journey. We should go tomorrow. By the way, I visited young McCarthy.'

'And what did you learn from him?'

'Nothing. At one point, I thought he was protecting the culprit but I am now convinced he is clueless. He seems like a nice person, but not very bright. You see, this fellow is madly in love with Miss Turner, but two years ago—before he really knew her, for she had been at a boarding school for five years—the idiot went and married a barmaid in Bristol. No one knows about this, but can you imagine how frustrating it must be to be constantly criticized for not doing the very thing he was dying to do, but absolutely could not.

'That is why he threw his hands up when his father forced him again into proposing to Miss Turner in their last quarrel.'

'Then again,' Holmes continued, 'James McCarthy has no income and his father would have disinherited him had he discovered the truth. In fact, James had spent the previous three days with his barmaid wife in Bristol. Remember this; it is important. However, good has come out of evil. Once the barmaid heard of Mr McCarthy's troubles, she wrote to him telling him that she already had a husband and, therefore, had no ties with him. I think that letter cheered up the young man quite a bit.'

'But if he's innocent,' I asked, 'who is guilty?'

'There is the question!' Holmes replied. 'We know the murdered man had an appointment that afternoon, and that the appointment could not have been with his son.

'The, victim called out, "Cooee!" before he knew of his son's return. Anyway, we shall discuss this further tomorrow, after we have been to Boscombe Pool.'

The next morning, we set out for Hatherley Farm with Lestrade and reached at nine o'clock.

'Mr Turner's condition has worsened,' Lestrade said.

'An elderly man, I suppose?'

'About sixty, but his years abroad ruined his health, which has been failing ever since. This tragedy has affected him very badly. He was an old friend of McCarthy's, and had even given him Hatherley Farm rent free.'

'Interesting!' Holmes said. 'And Turner helped McCarthy in a hundred other ways, has he not?'

'Really! Does it not strike you as strange that this McCarthy—who seemed to have so little, and been under such obligation to Turner—would simply assume that Turner would allow his son to marry Miss Turner, the heiress to the estate? Especially since Turner himself was against to the idea.'

Lestrade replied that he was still convinced of James McCarthy's guilt.

We soon reached Hatherley Farm, where we were shown in. At Holmes's request, the maid showed us the boots her master was wearing when he died, and also a pair of his son's. Holmes then measured both pairs of boots, and the three of us headed to Boscombe Pool, at the boundary between Hatherley Farm and Mr Turner's private park.

It was damp marshy ground, and there were many footprints, both upon the path and amid the short grass which surrounded it on either side. Sometimes, Holmes hurried on and sometimes, he stopped dead, and once he took a route into the meadow.

We could see Mr Turner's house above the woods lining the pool. On the Hatherley side, the woods grew very thick, and there was a narrow belt of soaking grass twenty paces across between the edge of the trees and the reeds that lined the lake.

Lestrade showed us where the body had been found. The ground was so soggy that I could plainly see where the man had fallen. Holmes—as I could see from his eager face and peering eyes—had seen many other things in the trampled grass. He ran round, like a dog picking up a scent, and then turned upon Lestrade.

'Why did you go to the pool?' he asked.

'I was fishing about, looking for a weapon. But how on earth—'

'That left foot of yours with its inward twist is all over the place. A mole could trace it, and there it vanishes among the reeds. I wish I had been here before they came like a herd of buffalo and splashed all over it. Patience Moran's party has covered all tracks for six or eight feet around the body. But here are three separate tracks of the same feet.'

He looked at the ground again with a magnifying lens, and said, 'Young McCarthy's feet show he walked twice, and ran swiftly once—for the soles are deeply marked and the heels hardly visible—probably when he saw his father on the ground. Here are the father's feet as he paced up and down. And the butt-end of the gun rested here, as the son stood listening.'

'Tiptoes!' Holmes said. 'Square, too, quite unusual boots! They come, they go, they come again—of course that was for the cloak. But where did they come from?'

He followed the track to a great beech tree. He lay down, and remained there, turning over leaves and dried sticks. He gathered up what appeared to be dust into an envelope and then re-examined the ground as well as the bark of the tree. He then picked up a jagged stone from the moss, carefully looked at it and kept it. Then, he followed a pathway through the woods until he came to the highroad.

'I will meet you at the carriage. I need to stop at Moran's house to write a note,' Holmes said to me.

Ten minutes later, we were on the carriage back to Ross, when Holmes handed Lestrade the jagged stone he had picked up earlier.

'Your murder weapon,' he said.

'You think so? There are no marks on it!'

'The grass was growing under it, so it had lain there only for a few days. It agrees with the injuries, and there is no sign of any other weapon.'

'And the murderer?'

'Is a tall man, left-handed, limps with the right leg, wears thick-soled shooting boots and a grey cloak, smokes Indian cigars, uses a cigar-holder and carries a blunt penknife. There are several other indications, but these should be enough for now.'

Lestrade laughed, doubtingly.

'Theories are good, but we have to deal with a hard-headed British jury,' he said.

'To each his own,' Holmes said. 'I shall tie up the loose ends this afternoon and be in London this evening.'

'You've already solved the mystery? Who was the criminal?'

'I have described the gentleman.'

'But who is he? I need a name before I can go hunting for a left-handed gentleman with a bad leg.'

'All right then, I will let you know before I leave,' Holmes said, as we dropped Lestrade at his lodgings before going to our hotel for lunch.

As the table was cleared, Holmes said, 'As I said before, two points struck me about young McCarthy's statement. One was that his father had cried, "Cooee!" before seeing him. The other was his dying remark about a rat.'

'He murmered several words, you understand, but that was all that caught the son's ear,' Holmes went on. 'Now, assuming the lad is telling the truth, the "Cooee!" was obviously not meant for the son, since he did not know he had returned from Bristol. He just happened to be within earshot. The "Cooee!" was meant to attract whoever it was that he was supposed to meet. But that is a clearly Australian cry, and one used between Australians. So the person he was meeting at Boscombe Pool had probably been in Australia.'

'And the rat?' I asked.

Holmes took out a piece of paper and unfolded it. It was a map of Victoria, Australia. He covered a part of it with his hands, and said, 'What do you read?'

'ARAT,' I read.

He removed his hand. 'And now?'

'Ballarat,' I read this time.

'That is the word the dying man uttered, but his son only heard the last two syllables. He was trying to utter the name of his murderer. So and so, of Ballarat.'

'Point three was the mysterious grey garment,' Holmes said. 'So, we are looking for an Australian from Ballarat with a grey cloak. And he must live in the area, since it can only be approached from the farm or the estate.

'Today's expedition gave me his height and other details that I shared with Lestrade.'

'I assume you guessed his height from the length of his stride, and that his boots left unusual prints. But the rest?' I asked.

'The left foot left a lighter impression than his right, meaning he put less weight upon it. Why? Because he limped,' Holmes said.

'But how do you know he is left-handed?'

'You yourself were struck by the nature of the injury as recorded by the surgeon. The blow was struck from immediately behind, and yet was upon the left side. Now, how can that be unless it were struck by a left-handed man?'

'He stood smoking a cigar behind the beech tree while the McCarthys argued. You know I can identify one forty different types of tobacco from ash, and thus knew the ash that I found near the tree came from an Indian cigar. I later found the cigar stump in the moss where he had tossed it. Since the end had not been in his mouth, he used a holder. The tip had been cut off, not bitten off, but the cut was not clean, so I deduced a blunt penknife.'

'Holmes, you have saved an innocent man! I see where all this points. The culprit is—'

'Mr John Turner,' announced the hotel waiter, ushering a visitor into our room.

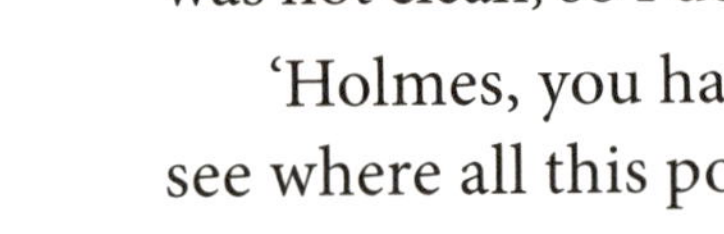

A strange and impressive man entered. His slow limping step and bowed shoulders made him appear frail, but his hard, deep-lined craggy features and his enormous limbs showed that he possessed unusual strength of body and of character.

His twisted beard, greyish hair and hanging eyebrows combined to give an air of dignity to his appearance, but his face was ashen, and his lips and the corners of his nostrils were tinged with blue. It was clear that he was very ill.

'Please sit down,' Holmes said gently. 'You received my note?'

'Yes, you said you wished to see me here to avoid scandal.'

'I thought people would talk if I came to you,' Holmes said.

'And why did you wish to see me?' Mr Turner looked wearily at my companion, as if he already knew the answer.

'Yes,' Holmes said, answering the look rather than the words. 'I know all about McCarthy.'

The old man sank his face in his hands.

'I would have spoken out if the court had decided against the young man,' he cried, 'I only kept quiet for my daughter's sake. It will break her heart when she hears that I am arrested.'

'It may not come to that,' said Holmes.

'What?'

'I'm not a policeman. I am only acting in your daughter's interests since she required my presence here. Young McCarthy must be got off, however.'

'I am dying,' old Turner said. 'I have had diabetes for years. And now, my doctor does not expect me to survive the month. However, I would rather die at home than in jail.'

Holmes picked up a pen and sat at the table, with a bundle of papers before him.

'Tell us the truth. I will write down the facts, and you can sign it. Watson here can witness it,' Holmes said. 'Then I can use your confession as the last resort to save young McCarthy. I promise not to use it unless it is absolutely needed.'

'Just as well. I doubt I shall live long enough to be taken to court, but it will spare Alice the shock. It will be a short tale,' Mr Turner said.

'One day, we held up a gold convoy. There were six guards and six of us, so it was a close call. We killed four men and lost three of our own, before we got the haul. I put my gun to the head of the wagon driver—the very same McCarthy—but spared him. I later wished I hadn't. His wicked little eyes were fixed on my face to remember every feature.

'We got away with the gold, and made our way to England as wealthy men. I parted from my friends and bought this estate, determined to settle down to a respectable life. I married, and though my wife died young, she left me my dear Alice. I turned over a new leaf, and all was going well. But then I met McCarthy again while I was on work in Regent Street. He hardly had a coat to his back or a boot to his foot, and threatened to have me arrested if I did not provide for his son and him.

'They have lived on my best land ever since. His

demands increased as Alice grew up, for he realized I would do anything to keep Alice from my past. Everywhere I turned, I saw his cunning face at my elbow. Eventually, he wanted the one thing I would not—could not—give him. He wanted Alice.

'You see, my ill health was common knowledge, and he wanted his son to inherit all my property. The boy is all right, but he is a McCarthy, so I stood firm. His father threatened me and I challenged him to do his worst. We were to meet at the pool to talk it over.

'He was talking with this son when I got there, so I smoked a cigar and waited behind a tree till he was alone. However, his words provoked me. He was urging his son to marry Alice without any regard to her desires. It maddened me to think of my daughter in the power of such a bad man. I was dying and desperate. My girl and my memory could be saved if I could just snap my bond with McCarthy. So I did it, Mr Holmes, and would do it again, if it would keep my girl safe from men like McCarthy.

'I killed him like he was a foul beast. His cries brought back his son, and I hid myself in the woods, but had to go back later to get my coat, which I had dropped. That is the whole story,' Mr Turner concluded.

'It is not for me to judge you,' Holmes said, as the old man signed the statement which had been drawn up. 'I hope we never have to expose your role in this.'

'I hope so too. But what do you intend to do?'

'Nothing, considering your health; you will be answering to a higher power than the courts soon enough. I will keep your confession a secret—whether you are alive or dead—unless McCarthy is criticized and attacked. In that case, I will be forced to use it.'

'Farewell, then,' said the old man seriously as he stumbled slowly from the room, 'and thank you for the peace you have given me.'

Holmes and I sat in silence for a long while.

'God help us!' said Holmes, eventually. 'Why does fate play such tricks with poor, helpless people? I never hear of such a case as this without thinking, "There, but for the grace of God, goes Sherlock Holmes".'

James McCarthy was ultimately set free on the strength of the objections that Holmes submitted to the defending counsel. Old Turner lived for seven months after our interview, but is now dead; and there is a strong likelihood that the son and daughter may come to live happily together, with no knowledge of the dark cloud which rests upon their past.

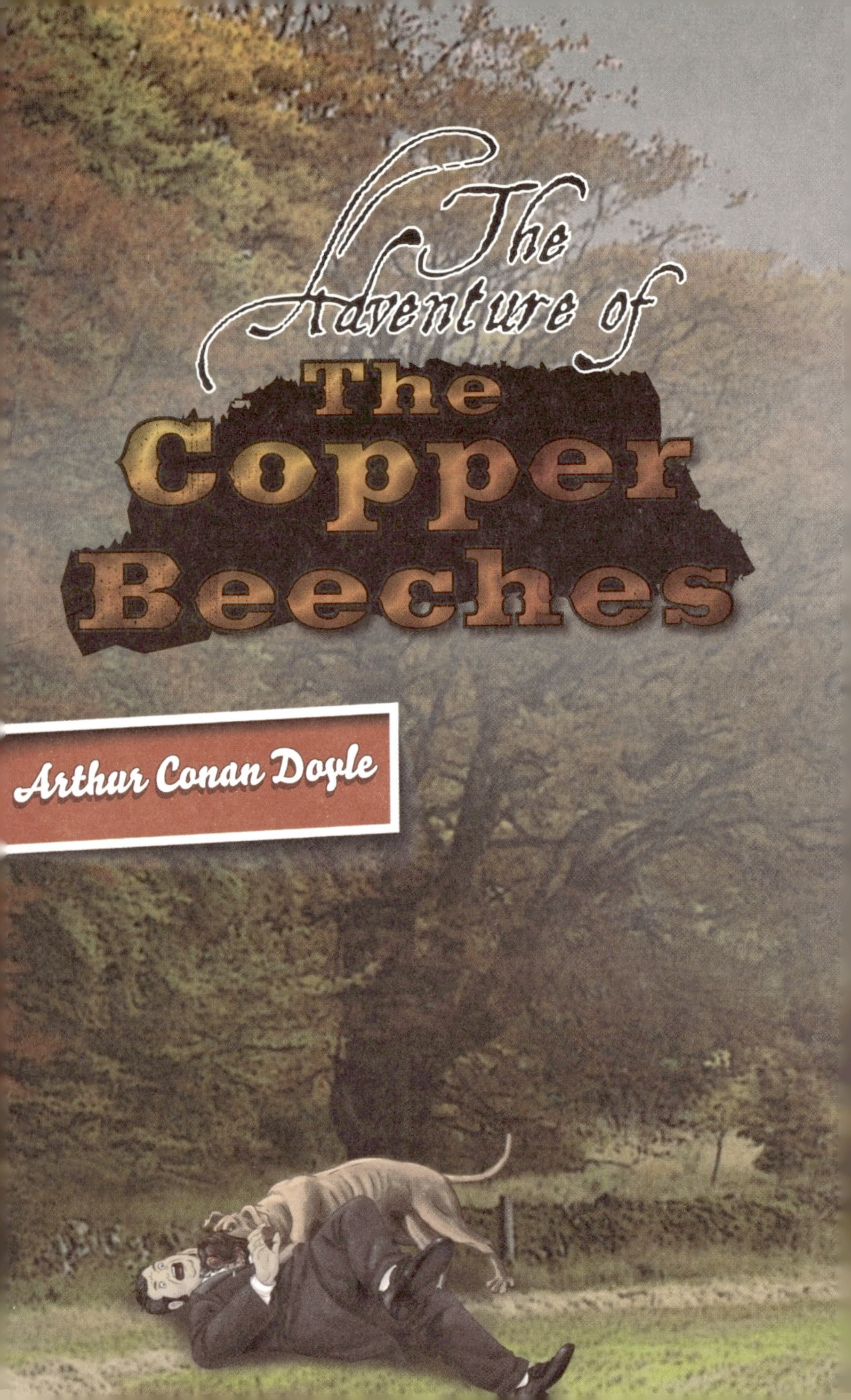
The Adventure of
The Copper Beeches
Arthur Conan Doyle

It was a cold foggy morning, and Holmes and I had just finished breakfast. As we sat in front of a warm fire at our Baker Street room, Holmes scolded me for decorating my reports of his cases with seemingly unimportant details that had helped him with his findings, rather than sticking to the hard facts. I thought, not for the first time, that my friend was being arrogant.

'I'm not arrogant,' Holmes said, reading my mind.

'Crime is common,' he said, 'but logic is rare. Therefore, I feel you should have focused on the logic than the crime. You made what should have been lectures into stories.'

'Then again, man—or at least criminal man—has lost all sense of originality. For instance, my own practice is developing into an agency for getting back lost pencils and advising young ladies. I think I have hit rock bottom. Just look at this note I received this morning!'

He tossed me a crumpled note, which read:

I am very anxious to consult you as to whether I should or should not accept a situation which has been offered to me as governess. I shall call at half-past ten tomorrow if I do not inconvenience you.

Yours faithfully,

Violet Hunter.

'Do you know the young lady?' I asked.

'No, but I wager that that is her at the door.'

'This may turn out to be more interesting than you think.'

Just then, the door opened and a young lady entered the room. She was plainly but neatly dressed, with a bright face, heavy brown hair and the quick manner of someone who has had to make her own way in the world.

'I am sorry for bothering you,' she said to Holmes, 'but I am hoping that you would be kind enough to tell me what I should do.'

'Take a seat, Miss Hunter,' Holmes said, rising. 'I shall be happy to try and help you in any way I can.'

He then settled himself, and we listened to her story.

'I have been a governess for five years,' Miss Hunter began, 'but my employer was transferred to America two months ago. He took his children with him, and I was left without a job. I ran newspaper advertisements, and responded to advertisements, but to no avail.'

She went on, 'The little money I had was running out quickly and I was at my wits' end.

I had taken to visiting a well-known agency for governesses, about once a week. When I went last week, Miss Stoper, the manager, was not alone in her office, which was unusual. With her was a huge man with a smiling face and multiple chins. As I entered, he gave a start, and turned quickly to Miss Stoper.

"That will do! I could not ask for anything better," he said to her, and rubbed his hands together quite cheerfully.

"You are looking for a position as a governess, miss?" he asked me.

'I replied, "Yes, sir."

"And what salary will you be wanting?"

"I had £4 a month in my last place."

'He threw his fat hands out into the air and cried, "How could anyone offer so small a sum to a lady with such attractions and accomplishments?"

"My achievements, sir, may be less than you imagine," I said. "A little French, a little German, music, and drawing—"

"Nonsense. The point is, do you not have the bearing of a lady? Then how could any gentleman ask you to accept anything under the three figures? Your salary with me, madam, would begin at £100 a year."

'As you can imagine, Mr Holmes, such an offer seemed too good to be true. But the gentleman seemed aware of my apprehensions. He took out a cheque book and began writing in it.

"It is also my habit to advance my employees half their salaries beforehand, so they may pay for expenses such as the journey and their clothes."

'I was very impressed by his thoughtfulness. Yet, something seemed fishy, and I did not want to commit myself.

"Where do you live, sir?" I asked.

"Hampshire. A lovely little country house called The Copper Beeches about five miles from Winchester."

"And, sir, what would my duties be?"

"One child, a dear little six-year-old. Oh, if you could see him killing cockroaches with a slipper. Smack! Smack! Smack! Three gone before you could wink!" He leaned back in his chair and laughed heartily.

'I was a little surprised at the nature of the boy's amusement, but the father's laughter made me think he was joking.

"So my sole duty would be to care for the boy?" I asked him.

"No, not the sole duty, young lady," he cried. "You will also help my wife in whatever she demands, provided her commands were such as a lady might with propriety obey."

"I should be happy to make myself useful."

"Quite so. In dress now, for example. We are fussy people, you know—fussy but kind-hearted. If you were asked to wear any dress which we might give you, you would not object to our little whim. Huh?"

"No," said I, considerably astonished at his words.

"Or to sit here, or sit there, that would not be offensive to you?"

"Oh, no."

"Or to cut your hair quite short before you come to us?"

'I could hardly believe my ears. As you may observe, Mr Holmes, my hair is quite luxuriant and of a rather peculiar tint of chestnut. It has been considered artistic. I could not dream of sacrificing it in such an off-hand manner.

"I am afraid that is impossible," I said. He had been watching me closely, and I saw a shadow pass over his face as I spoke.

"That is quite essential," he said.

'He went on, "My wife fancies it, and one cannot ignore ladies' fancies. Are you sure you won't cut your hair."

"No sir, I cannot."

"Very well then; that settles it. It is a pity because, in all other aspects, you would have done very well. In that case, Miss Stoper, I better meet a few more of your young ladies."

'Miss Stoper glared at me. "Do you wish us to keep looking for work for you?" she asked.

"Yes, please," I said.

"Well", she said, "it seems pointless. You refuse excellent offers in this casual manner, so you can hardly expect us to bother finding other opportunities for you. Good day, Miss Hunter." Then she rang a gong and I was shown out.

'Well, Mr Holmes, I returned to my lodgings, took stock of my finances and then began wondering if I had been too hasty to turn down the offer,' Miss Hunter said.

She went on, 'After all, these strange people were at least willing to pay. Very few governesses get paid £100 a year. Besides, I thought, short hair looks good on many people, so why not on me? Two days later, I was sure I had made a mistake. I had almost returned to ask if the position was still open when I received a letter from the gentleman himself.'

She showed us the letter. It read:

The Copper Beeches, Winchester.

Dear Miss Hunter,

Miss Stoper has very kindly given me your address, and I write to ask you if you have reconsidered your decision. My wife was impressed with my description of you and is very anxious that you should come. We are willing to give you £120 a year, so as to compensate for any inconvenience which our whims may cause you.

The letter continued:

My wife is fond of a particular shade of electric blue and would like you to wear such a dress indoors in the morning. However, you do not need to purchase one, as we have one belonging to my dear daughter Alice (now in Philadelphia), which I think would fit you. As regards your hair, it is no doubt a pity, but I must remain firm upon this point, and I only hope that the increased salary may recompense you for the loss. Your duties, as far as the child is concerned, are very light. Now do try to come, and I shall meet you at Winchester. Let me know your train. Yours faithfully,

Jephro Rucastle

'The letter convinced me to accept the offer. However, I would like your opinion before I take the final step,' Miss Hunter said to Holmes. 'What do you think?'

'If you have decided, then that settles it,' Holmes said. 'However, I admit I would not advise a sister of mine to accept such an offer.'

'What do you mean, Mr Holmes?' Miss Hunter asked.

'I cannot say, as I have no data. But perhaps you have formed some opinion?'

'Mr Rucastle seems nice enough. So the only possible answer is that his wife is mentally ill and instead of giving her to an asylum, he indulges her every whim.'

'That is possible,' Holmes said. 'Still, it does not seem like a nice household for a young lady.'

'But the money, Mr Holmes, the money!'

'Yes, the pay is good; a little too good, which makes me uneasy. Why would they pay £120 when they could have their pick for £40?'

'I thought that if you knew the circumstances, you would respond if I needed your help later.'

'Oh, you may depend on me. If you should find yourself in doubt or in danger—'

'Danger! Do you think I am in some danger?'

'I cannot define it. However, if you need me, send me a telegram day or night, and I shall be there.'

'That is enough,' Miss Hunter said, rising from her chair. 'I shall write to Mr Rucastle at once, sacrifice my hair tonight, and leave for Winchester tomorrow.'

She then thanked us and was on her way.

'She seems capable of taking care of herself,' I said.

'She would need to be,' Holmes said, seriously. 'I believe we will be hearing from her before long.'

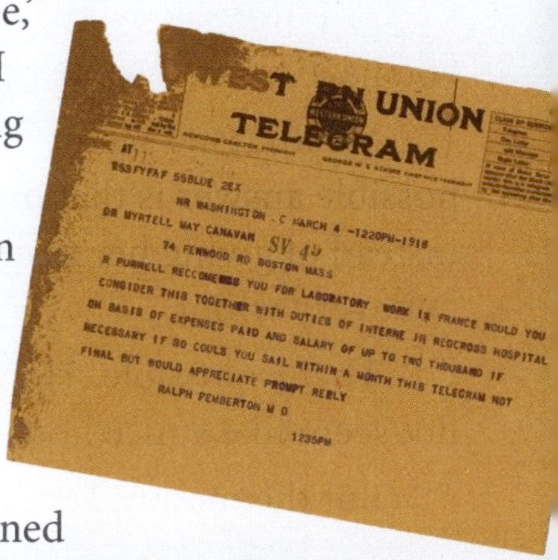


My friend's prediction was fulfilled a mere fortnight later. The telegram came late at night. I was preparing to go to bed. Holmes opened the yellow envelope, looked at the message, and threw it to me.

'Look up trains,' he said.

The summons was brief and urgent.

'Please be at the Black Swan Hotel at Winchester at noon tomorrow,' it said. 'Do come! I am at my wits' end. —Hunter.'

'There's one at half-past nine,' I said. 'It reaches Winchester at half-past eleven.'

'That will do very nicely,' he said.

Around eleven the next morning, we had crossed the Hampshire border. Holmes buried himself in the newspaper while I sat enjoying the view. The sun was shining very brightly, and yet there was an exciting nip in the air. All over the countryside, the little red and grey roofs of the farm-steadings peeped out from amid the light green of the new foliage.

'Are they not beautiful?' I cried.

But Holmes shook his head, seriously.

'You look at these scattered houses, and see their beauty. I look at them, and all I see is their isolation and the liberty with which crime may be committed there,' he went on.

'The dirtiest alleys in London are safer than the smiling beautiful countryside.'

'You horrify me!' I cried.

'The reason is obvious,' Watson said. 'Public opinion in the city can accomplish more than the law can in the countryside. There is no city lane

so dirty that the scream of a tortured child, or the thud of a drunkard's blow, does not cause sympathy among the neighbours. Thereafter, a single word of complaint can mean a prison sentence.'

'But these little houses are filled for most part with poor ignorant people who know little of the law. Think of the actions of horrible cruelty that may go on in such places, day in and day out, with no one finding out. Had Miss Hunter gone to live in Winchester, I would not fear for her.'

'It is the five miles of country which makes the danger. Still, it is clear she is not personally threatened.'

'Yes,' I said, 'if she can meet us at Winchester, she is free to get away. What do you think is the problem?'

'I cannot say for sure. We shall know more after we have spoken to Miss Hunter.'

We made our way to the Black Swan. There, we found the young lady—and the lunch she had ordered for us—waiting for us at a table.

'It is so kind of you both to come,' she said earnestly. 'I do not know what to do. Your advice will be helpful.'

'Do tell us what has happened to you,' Holmes said.

'I will, but I must be quick, for I have to be back by three. I got Mr Rucastle's permission to come into town, but he does not know my purpose.'

'Let us have it then,' Holmes said, bringing his long thin legs out towards the fire and composing himself to listen.

Miss Hunter began, 'It is only fair to say that, on the whole, I have not been mistreated by either Mr or Mrs Rucastle. However, I cannot understand them and am not at ease with them.'

'What can you not understand?'

'The reasons for their conduct. But let me start from the beginning,' Miss Hunter said.

'When I got here, Mr Rucastle took me to the Copper Beeches. The location of the house is very beautifully located with a clump of copper beeches immediately in front of the hall door. The house itself, however, is a large square block, whitewashed, but all stained and streaked with damp and bad weather.

'That evening, Mr Rucastle introduced me to his son and his wife, who—by the way—is not mad. She is a silent pale-faced woman, about fifteen years younger than her husband. I learnt that they had been married for seven years, and that he was a widower. His only child from his first marriage was the daughter in Philadelphia. Mr Rucastle later told me the girl had left for America since she did not get along with her stepmother.

'To be very honest,' Miss Hunter went on, 'Mrs Rucastle did not make much of an impression on me, either good or bad. She is devoted to her little son and her husband, who is kind to her in his bluff cheerful manner. On the whole, they seemed a happy couple, but the woman seems to have some secret sorrow. I have surprised her in tears more than once.

'At times, I think she is worried about her son, for I have never before seen so utterly spoiled and so ill-natured a little creature.

'He is small for his age with extremely large head. He spends his time either throwing tantrums or sulking. Making small creatures miserable seems to be his sole hobby, and he has a huge talent in capturing mice, little birds and insects. But I would rather not talk about the creature, Mr Holmes, and, anyway, he has little to do with my story.'

'Do not leave out any details, even if they seem unimportant,' Holmes said.

Miss Hunter picked up her story again.

'The servants—a man called Toller and his wife—are quite unpleasant. Toller is an uncultured man and is often drunk, but Mr Rucastle takes no notice of it. His wife is a tall and strong woman with a sour face. She is as silent as Mrs Rucastle, but much less friendly. Luckily, I do not have to interact with them much.

'My first two days at the Copper Beeches were quiet. On the third morning, after breakfast, Mr Rucastle addressed me after his wife whispered something in his ear.

"Thank you, Miss Hunter, for humouring our whims so far as to cut your hair. I assure you that it has not diminished your appearance one bit. We shall now see how you look in the electric-blue dress laid out upon your bed. Could you please put it on?"

'The dress was a strange shade of blue, made of an excellent material, but had obviously been worn before. It fit me perfectly. My employers seemed too delighted to see me in it. They were waiting for me in the enormous drawing room, which has three long windows. A chair had been placed close to the central window, with its back turned towards it. In this I was asked to sit, and then Mr Rucastle, walking up and down on the other side of the room,

began to tell me a series of the funniest stories that I have ever heard. I laughed until I was quite weary. Mrs Rucastle, however, never even smiled, but sat with her hands in her lap, looking sad and anxious. After an hour or so, Mr Rucastle suddenly said I could go and change my dress, and attend to little Edward.

'Two days later, the same thing,' Miss Hunter said. 'They ensured that my face was away from the window, so I was dying to see what was happening behind me. At first, I thought it was an impossible task, but I soon devised a method. I hid a small piece of glass in my handkerchief. The next time, in the midst of my laughter, I put my handkerchief up to my eyes, and looked behind me. I was upset, for there seemed to be nothing there. On my second try, I noticed a small bearded man in a grey suit, on the road outside. It is a busy road and there are usually people there, but this man was leaning against the railings and appeared to be looking in my direction.

'When I lowered my handkerchief, I found Mrs Rucastle's eyes fixed upon me. She said nothing, but I am convinced she figured out what I had done. She rose at once.

"Jephro," she said, "there is an unrelated fellow staring at Miss Hunter from the road."

"A friend of yours, Miss Hunter?" Mr Rucastle asked.

"No, I know no one in these parts."

"Dear me! How rude! Please turn around and wave him away."

'I did as I was told and, immediately, Mrs Rucastle pulled down the blind. That was a week ago. Since then, I have never been asked to wear the dress or sit in the window. I have also never seen the man again.'

Miss Hunter paused in her story and Holmes urged her to continue.

'This may have no bearing on the other incidents, but Mr Rucastle owns an enormous mastiff. The tawny animal is kept chained in an outhouse near the kitchen during the day and wanders the grounds freely at night. It is kept half-starved so as to make it more ferocious. Only Toller can control it. It is so aggressive that Mr Rucastle warned me not to step over the entrance at night.'

Miss Hunter jumped topics again.

'I have another curious incident to report. When I cut my hair off, I had placed the long coil at the bottom of my trunk. When I was unpacking, I opened a locked drawer and was shocked to

see my hair sitting there. I then went back to my trunk and found my own hair as I had kept it. I compared the two coils and found them to be identical in colour as well as thickness. I said nothing of the matter to the Rucastles.

'A few days after I had arrived there, I realized one wing of the house appeared to be uninhabited. The door that led there was usually locked. One day, however, while wandering there, I met Mr Rucastle coming out through this door, his keys in his hand. He looked anything but jovial. His cheeks were red, his brow was all crinkled with anger, and the veins stood out at his temples with passion. He locked the door and hurried past me without a word or a look.

'My curiosity roused, I walked round to the side from which I could see the windows of this part of the house. There were four of them in a row, three of which were simply dirty, while the fourth was shuttered up. They were evidently all deserted. As I walked up and down, looking at them occasionally, Mr Rucastle came out to me, looking as merry and jovial as ever.

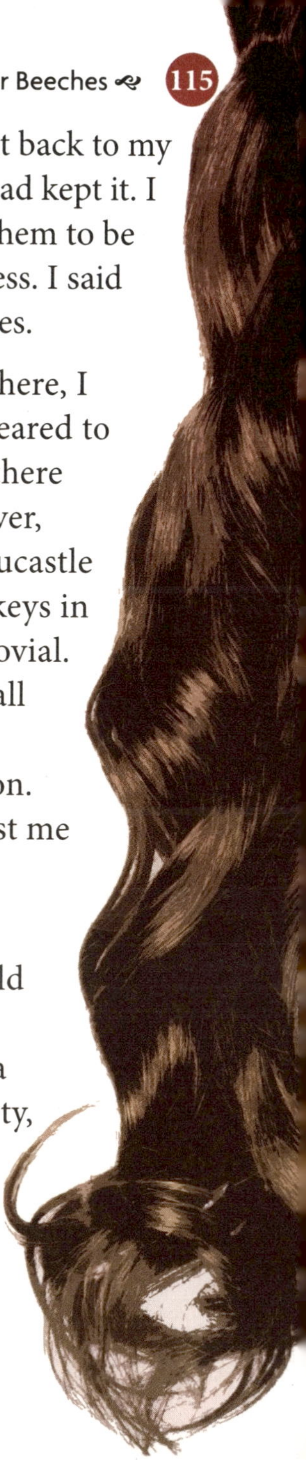

'He apologized for passing me by without speaking to me. I assured him I was not upset, and then casually remarked, "You seem to have a suite of spare rooms up there, and one of them has the shutters up."

'He looked a little startled, and said he had converted that room into a dark room since photography was one of his hobbies. "Dear me!" He cried in a jesting voice, "How observant you are!" However, there was no jest in his eyes when looked at me. I read suspicion and annoyance there, but no jest.

'Well, Mr Holmes, at that moment I decided I had to see what was in that room. It was more than mere curiosity that drove me. I had the distinct feeling that some good might come from my penetrating to this place. I began keeping a lookout for any chance to pass the forbidden door.

'I got my chance just yesterday. Apart from Mr Rucastle, the Tollers also frequent the lonely rooms. Toller was very drunk last evening and I found that he had left the key in the door. The Rucastles and their son were otherwise occupied, so I decided to grab the opportunity. I turned the key and slipped in.

'There was a little passage in front of me, leading to three doors. The first and third doors were open and led into empty, cheerless rooms. The centre door was barricaded and locked with a heavy padlock, and I guessed this went well with the darkened windows outside. Yet, I saw a glimmer of light beneath the door. Evidently, there was a skylight that let in some light.'

'I stood staring at the sinister door, wondering what lay beyond it. Just then, I heard footsteps from within the room and saw a shadow pass backwards and forwards against the little slit of dim light which shone out from under the door. I was terrified and ran out—straight into the arms of Mr Rucastle, who was waiting outside.'

"So, it was you! I guessed as much when I saw the door open," he said, smiling.

"I'm so frightened," I panted.

"And what has frightened you, my dear young lady?" he asked, soothingly. But his voice was a little too coaxing. I was immediately on my guard.

"I was foolish enough to wander in there on my own," I answered. "But it is so eerie, that I got frightened and ran out again. It is dreadful in there!"

"Only that?" he said, looking at me carefully.

"Why, what did you think?" I asked.

"Do you know why that door is kept locked?" Mr Rucastle asked me.

"I am sure that I do not know."

"It is to keep people out who have no business there. Do you see?" He was still smiling amiably.

"I am sure if I had known—"

"Well, then, you know now. And if you ever put your foot over that entrance again"—in an instant the amiable smile hardened into a grin of rage, and he glared down at me with the face of a demon—"I'll throw you to the mastiff."

'I was so terrified I do not know what I did. I suppose that I must have rushed past him into my room. I remember nothing until I found myself lying on my bed, trembling. I was frightened of the house, of the man, of the woman, of the servants, even of the child. They were all horrible to me.

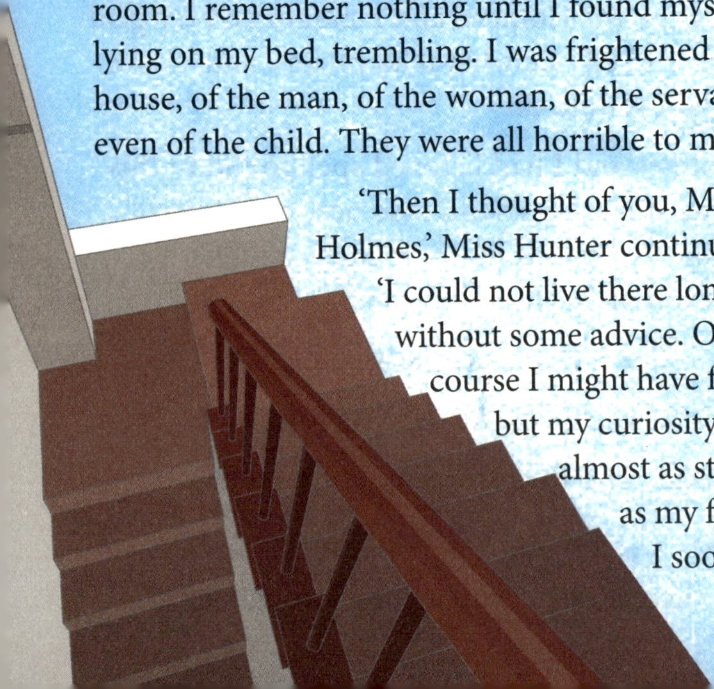

'Then I thought of you, Mr Holmes,' Miss Hunter continued. 'I could not live there longer without some advice. Of course I might have fled, but my curiosity was almost as strong as my fears. I soon decided to send you a wire. I put on my hat and cloak and went down to the office—about half a mile from the house. I then returned, feeling very much easier. I was assailed by a fear I approached the door lest the dog might be loose, but I remembered that Toller had drunk himself into a state of insensibility that evening. I knew that he was the only one in the household who had any influence with the savage creature, or who would venture to set him free. I slipped in and lay awake half the night, excited at the thought of your arrival.

'I got permission to come into Winchester this morning, but I must be back before three o'clock. The Rucastles will be away all evening, so I must look after the child. Now I have told you all my adventures, Mr Holmes, and I should be very glad if you could tell me what it all means, and, above all, what I should do.'

Holmes and I had listened spellbound to this amazing story. My friend rose now and paced the room, his hands in his pockets, a reflective expression on his face.

'Is Toller still drunk?' he asked.

'Yes. I heard his wife tell Mrs Rucastle.'

'Good. And Rucastles go out tonight?'

'Yes.'

'Is there a cellar with a good strong lock?'

'Yes, the wine cellar.'

'You have been very brave and sensible through all of this. But could you perform one more task?'

'I will try. What is it?'

'My friend and I will be at the Copper Beeches by seven o'clock. The Rucastles will be gone by that time and, hopefully, Toller will be incapable. That leaves just Mrs Toller. If you could send her into the cellar on some work, and then lock her in, you would facilitate matters immensely.'

'I will do it.'

'Excellent! We shall then get to the bottom of this! Of course, there is only one possible explanation. You have been brought here to act like someone, and that someone is imprisoned in that locked room. I have no doubt that the prisoner is, in fact, Alice Rucastle, who supposedly went to America. You were chosen, doubtless, since you were similar in height, figure and the colour of your hair. Hers had been cut off, very possibly during some illness, and so, of course, yours had to be sacrificed also.'

'The man on the road was undoubtedly some friend of Miss Rucastle's—possibly her fiancé—and no doubt, as you wore the girl's dress and were so like her, he was convinced from your laughter, whenever he saw you, and afterwards from your gesture, that Miss Rucastle was perfectly happy, and that she no longer wanted to see him. The dog is let loose at night to prevent him from trying to communicate with her. So much is fairly clear. The most serious point in the case is the child's behaviour.'

'How is that important?' I asked.

'My dear Watson! Just as you can tell a child's personality by studying that of its parents, the child's behaviour also speaks volumes of its parents' character. Considering that the child is cruel for cruelty's sake, it bodes evil for the poor girl who is in his parents' power.

'I am sure you are correct, Mr Holmes,' cried our client. 'Oh, let us lose not an instant in helping this poor creature.'

'We must be cautious since we are dealing with a devious man. We can do nothing until seven o'clock. It will not be long before we solve the mystery.'

We reached the Copper Beeches almost exactly at seven. The group of trees, with their dark leaves shining like burnished metal in the light of the setting sun, were sufficient to mark the house even had Miss Hunter not been standing smiling on the doorstep.

'Have you managed it?' Holmes asked as we entered.

A thudding noise came from somewhere downstairs.

'That is Mrs Toller in the cellar,' she said. 'Her husband lies snoring in the kitchen. Here are his keys, which are the duplicates of Mr Rucastle's.'

'Well done!' cried Holmes excitedly. 'Now lead the way, and we shall soon end this business.'

We soon came to the barricaded door Miss Hunter had described. Holmes tried various keys in the lock, but without success. His face clouded over when we realized there was no noise coming from inside.

'I hope we are not too late,' Holmes said. 'Watson, put your shoulder to it, and we'll see whether we cannot force our way in.'

The rickety old door gave way to our combined strength. We rushed inside. It was unfurnished except for a little pallet bed, a small table and a basketful of linen. The skylight above was open, and the prisoner gone.

'Ha!' said Holmes. 'He has guessed Miss Hunter's intentions and has carried off his victim.'

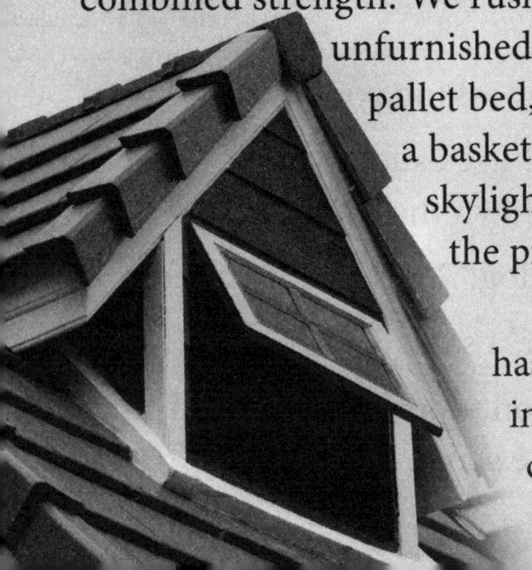

'But how?'

'Through the skylight,' Holmes said, as he swung himself up onto the roof. 'There's a long light ladder propped up against the eaves. That is how he did it.'

'But that ladder was not there when the Rucastles left the house,' Miss Hunter protested.

'Well, he must have come back and done it,' Holmes said. 'He is a wily man. In fact, it may be his footsteps we hear approaching. Watson, keep your pistol at the ready.'

He had hardly finished speaking when a burly man appeared at the door of the room with a heavy stick in his hand. Miss Hunter screamed and shrunk against the wall in fear, but Sherlock Holmes confronted him.

'You villain! Where is your daughter?'

The man looked around and then at the skylight.

'I should be the one asking you!' he called.

'Thieves and spies! I've caught you now!' he yelled as he clattered down the stairs.

'He's gone for the dog!' Miss Hunter cried.

'I have my revolver,' I said.

'Better close the front door,' Holmes said, and we all rushed down the stairs.

We had hardly reached the hall when we heard the baying of a hound, and then a dreadful scream of agony. An elderly man with a red face and shaking limbs came staggering out at a side door.

'My God!' he cried. 'Someone has let the dog out. It's not been fed for two days. Quick, quick, or it'll be too late!'

Holmes and I rushed out, with Toller behind us. The huge hungry animal had buried its black muzzle in Rucastle's throat, and he screamed and writhed upon the ground. Running up, I blew its brains out, and it fell over. We managed to separate man and dog and carried Rucastle, alive but horribly injured, into the house. We laid him upon the drawing room sofa, and dispatched Toller to inform his wife. We were all assembled round him when the door opened, and a tall gaunt woman—Mrs Toller—entered the room.

'Mr Ruscastle let me out when he came back. Ah, Miss, it is a pity you didn't let me know what you were planning, for I would have told you that your pains were wasted.'

Mrs Toller then began to fill in the gaps of our story.

'Miss Alice was never happy at home, not since her father remarried. Her mother had left her some money but she just left everything in Mr Rucastle's hands. Then she met Mr Fowler at a friend's house, and things got worse. Realizing that a husband would ask for all that the law would give him, her father tried to put a stop on it. He wanted her to sign a paper, so that whether she married or not, he could use her money. When she wouldn't do it, he kept on worrying her until she got brain fever.'

Mrs Toller continued, 'For six weeks, she was at death's door, but finally got better, worn to a shadow, and with her beautiful hair cut off, but her young man stuck by her.'

'Mr Rucastle then, I presume, took to this system of imprisonment?' Holmes interrupted, as the matter became clearer.

'Yes, sir.'

'And brought Miss Hunter down to get rid of Mr Fowler?'

'That was it, sir.'

'But Mr Fowler—being a persevering man—met you, and convinced you to help him. Thereafter, he made sure that your husband would remain drunk, and you placed the ladder at the side of the house as soon as your master went out.'

'That is what happened,' Mrs Toller said, just as the doctor and Mrs Rucastle arrived.

'I'm sure we owe you an apology, Mrs Toller,' Holmes said, before suggesting we escort Miss Hunter back to London.

And thus was solved the mystery of the evil house with the copper beeches in front of the door. Mr Rucastle survived, but was kept alive solely through the care of his devoted wife. They still live with their old servants. Mr Fowler and Miss Rucastle were married the day after their flight, and he now holds a government job in the island of Mauritius. As to Miss Violet Hunter, she has met with huge success as the head of a private school at Walsall.

# Other Titles *in the* Series

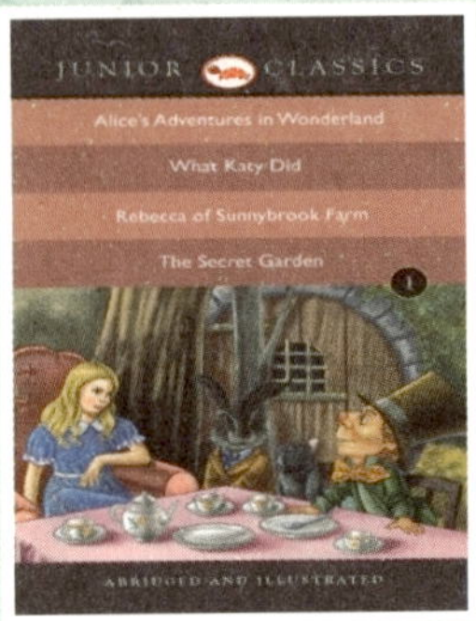


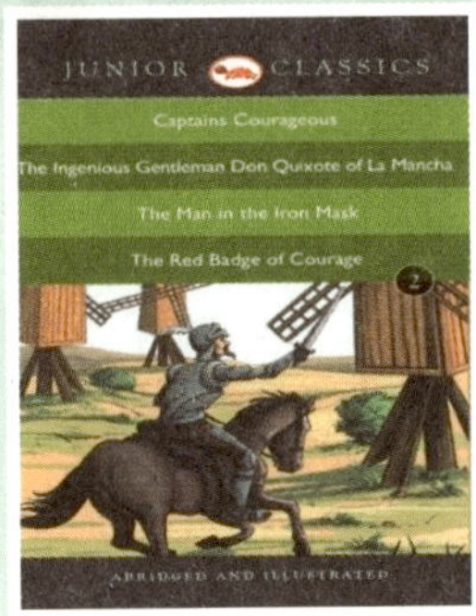


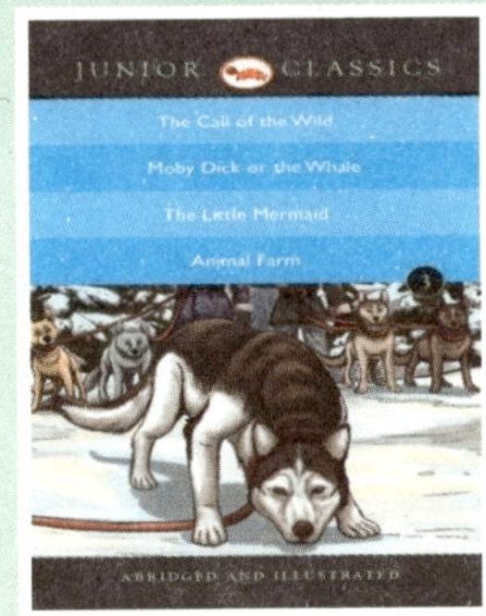

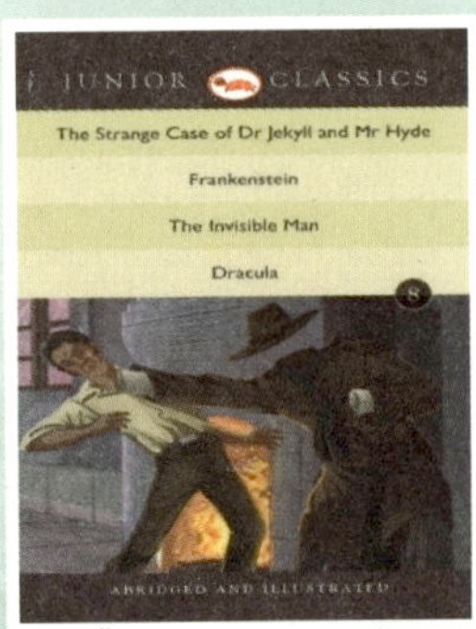


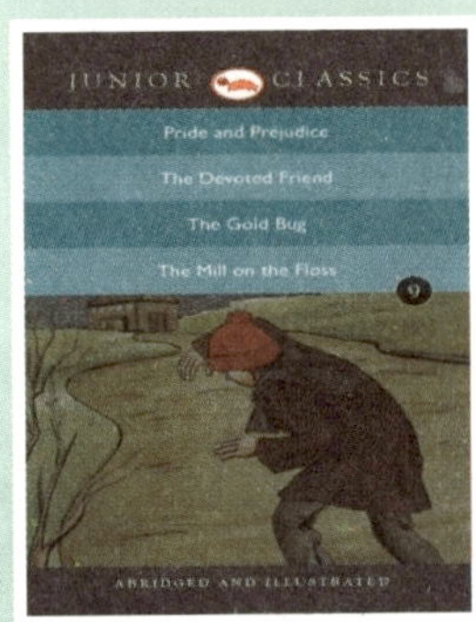